A Full-Bodied Love

by

Amber Cross

Love in the Kingdom, Book Four

A Full-Bodied Love

Cover Art by *Debbie Taylor*

The Wild Rose Press, Inc.
PO Box 708
Adams Basin, NY 14410-0708
Visit us at www.thewildrosepress.com

Publishing History
First Edition, 2022
Trade Paperback ISBN 978-1-5092-4213-9
Digital ISBN 978-1-5092-4214-6

Love in the Kingdom, Book Four
Published in the United States of America

"If you're running from the law, you've come to the wrong place."

A woman leaning out of the town clerk's service window pointed to the police department across the hall. She wore a black felt witch's hat, and orange pumpkins dangled from her ears, as brilliant as the smile on her face.

Well, well, well.

"It's not the cops I need," he admitted, approaching the window and thrusting his hand out in greeting. "I don't believe I've had the pleasure. Roger Plankey."

"Lisa Kirkpatrick."

Her skin was soft against his work-roughened palm, her beautifully manicured nails a sharp contrast to his blunt-tipped square fingers. Halloween decorations sparkled on the black-painted ovals, but nothing shone from her left ring finger. He checked.

"Are you new here, Lisa?"

"I'm the deputy clerk. I work when Maisie needs a day off."

"Ahh, that would explain why we haven't met before." Reluctantly, he took his hand back to retrieve paperwork from the inside pocket of his canvas barn jacket. "I've got a bunch of vehicles to register." He passed the documents through the window, letting his gaze wander over her pretty face while she scanned them. Brown hair curled against the brim of her witch's hat and caressed the nape of her neck. Thick eyelashes feathered high apple cheeks, and when they lifted, her hazel eyes reminded him of spring rain on the meadow.

Praise for Amber Cross and...

PRECEDENT FOR PASSION:
"...what a well written story that kept my interest until the end...it is almost like being there and watching the story unfold..."

~Barj70, Bookbub

~*~

TENDER POSSESSION:
"Two people could never be more different, culturally, physically, personality-wise, yet Cross creates a distinctive and undeniable chemistry between the two main characters of her book. Everyone deserves a Romney in their lives."

~Susan Hutchinson, Author

~*~

OPEN DOOR TO LOVE:
"Be prepared to keep turning the pages, especially when they sizzle. Ms. Cross has created flawed characters who stride through the story without forgetting a rich texture of the supporting cast..."

~Ellen, Bookbub

Dedication

For Pooh.
I hope Heaven welcomed you
with blaring rock music and bright rainbow colors.

~

Thanks to my farmer cousin, Colleen,
for answering questions on modern dairying.

~

A very special thanks to the ladies at
the Spina Bifida Association of Greater New England
for helping me bring Lisa's story to life.

~

To learn more, please visit: https://sbagreaterne.org

Author's Note

Full-bodied means to be heady, mellow, lusty,
mature, potent, rich, and strong.
I hope this love story represents those elements.

Chapter One

Roger Plankey was man enough to admit he looked over his shoulder before ducking inside the Somerset town offices on Saturday morning. He wasn't normally paranoid, but after three weeks of being pursued by a reality-show contestant bent on claiming him for herself, he wasn't taking any chances.

"If you're running from the law, you've come to the wrong place."

A woman leaning out of the town clerk's service window pointed to the police department across the hall. She wore a black felt witch's hat, and orange pumpkins dangled from her ears, as brilliant as the smile on her face.

Well, well, well.

"It's not the cops I need," he admitted, approaching the window and thrusting his hand out in greeting. "I don't believe I've had the pleasure. Roger Plankey."

"Lisa Kirkpatrick."

Her skin was soft against his work-roughened palm, her beautifully manicured nails a sharp contrast to his blunt-tipped square fingers. Halloween decorations sparkled on the black-painted ovals, but nothing shone from her left ring finger. He checked.

"Are you new here, Lisa?"

"I'm the deputy clerk. I work when Maisie needs a day off."

"Ahh, that would explain why we haven't met before." Reluctantly, he took his hand back to retrieve paperwork from the inside pocket of his canvas barn jacket. "I've got a bunch of vehicles to register." He passed the documents through the window, letting his gaze wander over her pretty face while she scanned them. Brown hair curled against the brim of her witch's hat and caressed the nape of her neck. Thick eyelashes feathered high apple cheeks, and when they lifted, her hazel eyes reminded him of spring rain on the meadow.

"This should only take a few minutes."

With a quick smile she turned to the computer on her desk.

"Hey, Slick, what you up to?"

"About five eleven, last time I checked," he replied to Ardell Stevens as the selectwoman emerged from her office down the hall. Ardell had been the high school physical education teacher before she took early retirement to nurse her husband through his last months with ALS. She was twenty years older than Roger, but they'd become friends through an informal grief group. "How 'bout yourself?"

"You know, same old, same old. I was wondering if you'd be interested—" She didn't get to finish her sentence because the door behind him blew open, and a waft of heavy perfume preceded the arrival of one crazy contestant from the reality show being filmed up at Somerset Gables Resort.

"There you are!" The predatory blonde sidled up next to him and looped her arm through his elbow as if she had a right to. "I've been looking all over for you." With a pout that probably worked on younger, more-gullible men, she said, "The crew has given us the night off, and I was hoping you could take me for a drive. Maybe show me some more of Vermont's Northeast Kingdom?"

Roger shook his head and extricated himself from her hold. "No can do." He slid to the other side of the service window, putting the ledge between them. "I've got a date with Lisa here."

To her credit, the deputy clerk's eyes widened, but she didn't contradict him.

"Oh." Blondie glanced at the black hat and orange pumpkin earrings, clearly disappointed. "Well, maybe some other time, then."

He didn't say anything because there was never going to be another time.

Laughing a little nervously at the awkward silence, she smiled at Lisa and Ardell without really looking at them, gave him a flirty wave, and let herself out of the office.

Ardell whistled. "Close call."

"You're telling me." He shuddered dramatically. "I think you were trying to ask me something before we got interrupted?"

"Oh yeah." A phone rang inside the selectmen's office, and she started down the hall, saying over her shoulder, "Card party starts tonight. You in?"

"Well, that depends on my date. Whadya say, Lisa?"

"You don't have to pretend now." She slid a pen and forms from the printer across the shelf for him to sign. "I'm pretty sure she left the parking lot."

"Who's pretending?" After adding his John Hancock in all the right places, he pulled his wallet from his back pocket and extracted a number of bills to cover the cost. "I'm asking you out on a date. Dinner and some kitty whist. Can I pick you up at six o'clock?"

She didn't answer him. Instead, she handed over his change and renewal paperwork before pushing away from the ledge on her side of the window. Holding her hands out at her sides as if she were a game-show hostess displaying a prize. Only she was showing him the wheelchair she sat in, hidden from his view until now. He could tell this wasn't the first time she'd introduced herself this way, and he wondered just how many douchebags had turned her down because of it.

He wasn't a douchebag, and she wasn't getting out of a date that easily. "Don't think I'm taking my invitation back just because you're a little heavier to *pick up* than the average gal."

"I'm hardly a gal."

"No, I'd say you're all woman and full of excuses at the moment. If you don't want to go with me, just say so, and I'll stop pestering you."

A blush colored her cheeks, and her eyes might have misted up a little, but it could also be the distance between them or the fluorescent lights overhead.

"Okay." She wheeled her chair closer to the window. "But I'll drive myself."

"Ah, so you're an independent woman. I can appreciate that."

"Where should I meet you?"

"Somerset Grange Hall." He tucked the change into his wallet, stuffed it in his back pocket, took the paperwork, and slid it inside his coat. Touching the brim of his John Deere cap with one hand, he winked at her and said, "Six o'clock. I'll be waiting for you."

Once outside on the walkway, he scanned the area

to make sure the wannabe bride wasn't lurking on the steps of the library or hiding around the corner of the volunteer fire department. It appeared safe. Still, he kept an eye out for her while climbing into his pickup truck and reversing out of the parking lot.

The vehicle wasn't made for speed, but he could probably lose a tail if he had to. Not that it would matter. The cast and crew of the marriage-market reality show knew where he lived.

"But they wanted to film an episode on a *real* Vermont dairy farm," his sister, Linda, had reasoned after announcing she invited them to visit. "I'll be there to show them around. You won't have to do a thing. Just go about your business and pretend they're not even there."

Easier said than done. Unlike visits from first graders or the 4-H club, these were tourists. Twenty-five women on the make with an entire entourage of directors, producers, camera operators, and makeup artists. They did nothing *but* get in the way. And it hadn't ended when they left the farm three weeks ago.

Blondie seemed to pop up whenever he went into town.

She would either get a clue or she wouldn't, and if the latter turned out to be the case, he'd deal with it. For now, he'd do his best to avoid her whenever possible and think about more important things, like his date with the intriguing Lisa Kirkpatrick.

She must be new to Somerset. He didn't have the most active social life, but his sister ran the diner, and his younger son was tapped into the dating "scene," for lack of a better description, yet they hadn't met before. He hadn't even heard about her. Surprising, because

Somerset had a three-to-one ratio of men to women, so any new female was a kitchen-table topic.

"Uncle Roger!"

His truck windows were no better than cheesecloth when it came to that high-pitched squeal.

Darcy frantically waved a car wash sign from the lawn of Somerset Academy.

How could he resist? Flipping the directional switch to signal a turn, he pulled into the school parking lot, and she raced over to the truck, long brown hair flying out behind her. Instead of waiting for him to roll down the windows, she opened the passenger door and leaned inside the cab as soon as he came to a stop.

"What's up, pumpkin?"

"Seriously?" She rolled her eyes dramatically, letting him know the nickname was old. Or maybe that was young, since she complained, "I am a teenager, you know."

"Duly noted."

"So maybe it's time to use my name. You know, the one on my birth certificate?"

He screwed his face up as if considering her suggestion, only to shake his head and grin. "Nah, I have a *thing* for pumpkins." In pies. In muffins. In fact, he even liked them dangling from a certain woman's ears.

"You're impossible!"

"Is that why you stopped me? To tell me that?"

"No, I called you over to get your truck washed. We're raising money for a band-and-chorus trip to Montreal."

"You could go there any day of the week. Just ask your father to take you." His brother, Glen, worked over the border as a cybersecurity expert for international banks.

"You're missing the whole point. C'mon, the line is over there." She waved toward the circular drive behind her where students worked with buckets, hoses, and sponges on a bright-green hatchback. The water sluicing over the car reminded him of spring rain on the meadow. Which reminded him of a certain lady he was meeting at six o'clock.

Might as well get his truck washed so Lisa wouldn't think he was careless about equipment maintenance.

"You've got yourself another customer."

Darcy closed the door and stepped away from the vehicle.

He pulled in behind the Volkswagen, only waiting the length of one song on the radio before it was his turn. While the kids covered his truck in suds, some using stools and mops to reach the top of the roof, he went through his to-do list for the day. *Make a dump run. Stack wood. Repair the side door on the small barn where a greedy river rat tried chewing its way into the grain bin. Milk the cows, of course. Take a shower and get polished up before supper at the Grange.*

He hadn't been out with a woman in months. Not since July and that was an arranged, rounding-off-the-numbers kind of thing. His sister-in-law, Abby, had had a friend visiting from Rutland, and she would have been the odd single woman out for dinner at The Gables, so he'd agreed to escort her. No pressure, which was good, because they had no chemistry. He couldn't even remember what she looked like now. Straw-colored hair. Blue eyes. Or maybe they were brown. They definitely weren't hazel green.

Darcy yanked the passenger door open again. "That'll be five bucks or whatever you want to donate." She held out an open clarinet case like a collection plate at church.

He shifted on the seat to get at his wallet, withdrew a ten spot, and added it to the small pile of cash.

"Thanks, Uncle Roger."

"You're welcome, pumpkin."

****

Finally! By the time the clock on the wall struck two, Lisa's pulse was synced to the *tick-tick-tick* of the second hand. She had counted down each movement of the last half hour when no customers came in. Ardell was long gone. She couldn't ask the selectwoman about Slick or how he came by that name, so she had nothing but the clock for company while she vacillated between excitement and trepidation.

Now she could finally call the one person whose advice she desperately needed.

"What's up, buttercup?" her best friend Jonnie answered on the second ring.

"I have a date!"

Okay, she hadn't meant to shout it for the whole neighborhood to hear, but the phone was in her lap while she wheeled down the sloped sidewalk to her handicapped parking spot.

"Should we take out an ad in the *Somerset Reporter*?"

"Don't bother. You could probably hear me up on the mountain." The novelty of the event and waiting four agonizing hours to share the news had made it impossible to contain.

Jonnie laughed at her nervous admission. "Give me all the details."

"A guy came in to register his vehicles," she began in a quieter tone, hitting the key fob to unlock her car.

"And?"

"Hold on." She opened the door, tossed her purse into the passenger seat, then put her phone on the dash and started the engine so she could continue their conversation through the hands-free link. "I've never met him before, and I think he has a stalker, because he told this lady I was his date."

Standing, she leaned against the car while squeezing the wheelchair flat between her palms. "When she left, he said he wasn't taking the invitation back, and—hold on again."

She heaved the wheelchair over the console onto the folded rear seats and lowered herself into the driver's side. A little out of breath from the exertion, but mostly from excitement, she closed the door and picked up the phone, panting. "And now I'm going to a card party. Some game called kitty, or whisk, something like that. And supper at the Grange hall."

"Woo-hoo! I want to know all about it, but David needs my help with the reality-show people. Can I call you back when we get done?"

"Sure thing."

The drive to her house wasn't a long one. The town offices were just off Circle Row, a two-lane ring road connected to the town common by side streets fanned out like spokes in a wheel. Little kids learned Somerset geography by memorizing how many spokes there were between starting points and destinations. Old folks used them when giving directions. "Take the third side road past the church," or "Supermarket is five roads after you come up from 114A." Nobody used the actual street names.

Lisa had thought it was an absurd system when she moved here two years ago. Now she went up onto the common, circled right until the fourth spoke, and turned right again onto Pleasant Street as if hypnotized. By the time she reached the top of the hill and the entrance to Somerset Place, she couldn't remember a single detail of the trip.

The jarring ring of her cellphone abruptly pulled her from that trance. When her sister's name and number flashed across the car's dashboard screen, she hit the decline button. "No rain on my parade, thank you very much."

In fact, not a single cloud hung over the housing complex sprawled across the hillside before her. A wide boulevard curled around and between a dozen pristine cottages. Neatly trimmed walkways ended at steps clustered with potted mums, and seasonal wreaths adorned front doors, letting everyone know they were welcome, when in reality security cameras were everywhere.

A dead spot was also at the beginning of the drive, but as soon as she cleared it, her phone rang again. This time Jonnie's name showed on the dashboard screen, and she almost shouted, "Accept call," while hitting the button to do so.

"Okay, what do you need?" Jonnie asked without preamble.

"An hour's worth of advice, but maybe you can just talk me down off this cliff I'm on."

"Is he good-looking?"

"Prettiest blue eyes on the planet." Like her car's paint job, glinting in the autumn sunshine before she parked beneath the carport attached to her craftsman-style home. "And a great voice. Great smile."

"Is he crazy?"

"What? No! I mean, he seemed normal, except for telling the woman we had a date."

"Does he have a name?"

"Hold on." Too keyed up to sit still for this conversation, she stepped out onto the driveway and put both hands on the roof of her car while continuing to talk through the stereo. "Roger Plankey." A good name, she thought, strong and sturdy. Much better than Slick.

"The dairy farmer."

"You know him?"

"We've met a couple of times. He owns the place by the bridge on 114A."

Lisa stretched her spine and visualized the property. A long driveway separated acres of hayfield rolling from the edge of the state route to a hilltop lined with venerable maple trees. The farm buildings themselves were on the other side of the ridge. She had seen the rooftops from the bridge where Route 114A ended at 114, and cows were pastured on that side of the property.

"He's a widower with two grown sons. His sister, Linda, owns the Townline Diner across from the farm," Jonnie continued, "and his brother, Glen, is married to David's sister, Abby. You met him at our wedding."

She remembered a tall, lean man with dark hair and blue eyes. The brothers shared the same coloring, but Roger was clean-shaven, more muscular, and closer to average in height.

11

"The Plankeys have been here for at least three generations, maybe longer."

This was all news to her, but in the way of New England courtship traditions since colonial times, no date was properly vetted until their family's reputation was established, so she was glad to have the information. It helped allay her concerns over his name—Slick.

"So you have a date with a hunky man who has a great smile, works hard and pays his bills, has a modicum of intelligence, and is interested in you."

She knew what Jonnie was doing, and it worked. For the first time since meeting him that morning, she relaxed. "Yeah. I do."

"We'd better get started, then. I only have half an hour before the boys wake up from their nap. So what are you going to wear?"

Chapter Two

She finished her outfit with barely enough time left to brush her teeth, freshen her makeup, and spritz on a light mix of floral and citrus notes that reminded her of a lazy summer afternoon. Something she liked to imagine on nights like this when the sunset robbed the earth of so much heat even the stars went into hiding.

That bitter dark turned out to be her friend. Finding the main parking lot full, she claimed a spot across from the hall in an overflow lot that was more a big open patch of dirt than anything. That side of the road had no lights, so while she could see the main entrance, no one noticed her.

This gave her a chance to observe Roger where he stood at the bottom of the access ramp beneath the lone streetlight. She could admit now to having been worried he'd come to his senses and back out of their date. He had no way to let her know if he changed his mind, since he didn't have her phone number, and images of herself sitting outside the hall waiting for a man who never showed had kept her on edge even as she got ready this afternoon.

Yet here he was in his brown canvas jacket, denim jeans, and a plaid flannel shirt. Today's John Deere cap had been replaced with one bearing the Montreal Canadiens logo, the red C winking at her each time he dipped his head to greet people entering the hall. She only recognized it because a block of game tickets had been donated to the hospital's annual fundraiser.

A gust of icy wind whistled down the empty roadway between them. Roger flipped the collar of his shirt and jacket up against the cold and looked out over the main parking lot. Probably searching for her. Maybe wondering if she was going to show up.

Not wanting to keep him waiting, she hauled her wheelchair out of the backseat and snapped it open. A rough section of cold patch took up half the paved road, so she rolled in a wide circle around it, placing her farther from the building and still out of his line of vision.

Through the ramp railings she watched his interactions with others.

"Gonna stand out here all night, or are you coming to dinner?" Chief Price asked, hitching her pants up over her stout form, made even stockier by the weapons and various tools strapped around her middle.

"I'll be in," he replied without explanation.

Lisa liked the policewoman, but Roger didn't elaborate, and she liked that even more. Something told her he was a man who kept his own counsel, and private business remained private. Since most of her work at the hospital was confidential, she appreciated his reserve.

Still, it would only be a matter of time before the residents of Somerset knew about their date if the local hotline wasn't broken.

Gabe Allen proved it was in good working condition when he stepped onto the ramp with his son Preston. "Ardell says you invited Lisa from the town-clerk's office."

"Did she now?"

Ardell had never had any children, and as a widow, she had a lot of time on her hands to speculate and gossip, so Lisa wasn't surprised. Or even upset she'd shared the news with her fellow selectman.

Gabe grinned at Roger's non-reply. "Well, good for you." Shifting a crockpot from one arm to the other, he took Preston's hand and started up the ramp, adding, "She's a nice woman."

Lisa was about to shout a loud, "Thank you!" until she heard another voice.

"You clean up good, Slick."

"Hey, Ardell."

The selectwoman had come around the corner of the building while Lisa rolled up the sloped road toward the low end of the ramp. From her position below them, her mouth watered at the warm smell of brownies wafting from a foil-covered pan in the woman's arms.

"I only told Gabe."

"It's okay." He went up the ramp ahead of her and pulled the door open.

Ardell nodded sharply, took a breath like she was going to say something else, then caught sight of Lisa rounding the end of the ramp and ducked inside.

Lisa rolled to a stop and admired his rugged good looks for a moment before announcing herself. "Hey, mister, are you looking for a date?"

****

Hello.

Roger's spine tingled, and he stood a little straighter. His pulse kicked up a notch.

He had half expected her to bail on him. A strange man asking her out as a shield against another woman's

15

avaricious attentions? No one would have blamed her if she decided this was a mistake.

He certainly hadn't made one.

A nimbus of gold from the streetlight surrounded her where she sat at the bottom of the ramp. Thick, lush curls framed her face, and her wide eyes sparkled; a cheeky smile accompanied her next words. "May I escort you to dinner?"

Ambling down the wooden slope to meet her, he matched her teasing tone. "I think that's supposed to be my line."

"Then my answer is yes."

He offered his elbow, and she slid her gloved hand along his sleeve. He liked the weight and warmth of her hold even through his jacket and shirt, only belatedly realizing she couldn't wheel herself up the ramp one-handed. "How is this going to work?"

"Maybe you could push me instead?"

"Sounds like a plan." Reluctantly he removed her hand from his arm, placed it in her lap, and propelled her wheelchair up the incline. A soft, womanly scent like something from his mother's flower garden wafted up to his nostrils. For a moment he considered turning around and taking her someplace with more privacy, but they had already reached the top, and someone inside held the door open for them.

Any chance of alone time vanished even before a familiar high-pitched voice exclaimed, "It's the Halloween lady!"

Darcy sat at a table in the vestibule beneath the golden sheaf sign of the Grange, tickets in her hand and a metal cash box open in front of her. On seeing him behind Lisa, she showed no surprise, probably thinking they happened to arrive at the same time. "Hey, Uncle Roger."

"Hey, pumpkin, how'd the car wash turn out?"

"Great! We got enough for the music trip. We're going in two weeks, so we can get shopping done before Black Friday. Not that it's Thanksgiving in Canada, so it doesn't really matter that much, but we still planned around people traveling then."

"How'd you get roped into doing this tonight?"

"Community service credit for school." Her bright-blue eyes took in his hand still on the back of Lisa's wheelchair. A puzzled look crossed her face, followed by the inevitable curiosity, then her mouth fell open on an "oh" of discovery. "You two are here together?"

Roger tapped the bottom of her chin with a bent knuckle. "Close it, or you'll catch flies."

Pink cheeked, she was uncharacteristically at a loss for words.

"I'm Lisa Kirkpatrick," Lisa said into the breach, "and, yes, your uncle invited me here for dinner and a card party. Is pumpkin your real name, or should I call you something else?"

Rolling her eyes and shooting him a long-suffering look, his niece said, "Darcy. Only *he* calls me by a vegetable name."

"Fruit."

"What?" Both females looked to him for explanation.

"Pumpkins are fruits, not vegetables."

"Whatever." Darcy waved her hand to dismiss his clarification, already rebounding to focus on Lisa. "You are going to be home tomorrow, right? We're trick-or-treating from three to five, and everybody has your house on the list. It's the best, Uncle Roger, and she's in a neighborhood—you know, an actual neighborhood with more than one house nearby—so we can get a bunch of candy all at the same time, but her house is still the best because she gives whole candy bars, not the little cheap ones or those religious pencils and Bible verses like the lady down the road, but—"

"Who would want a scripture lesson on Halloween, anyway?" Lisa's question forced his niece to take a breath.

"Exactly!"

"Think we can buy a couple of tickets?" Roger interjected before Darcy could get started again. "You know, since we're standing here and everything."

"Sitting and standing, you mean. Oh! Aunt Linda dropped off your crockpot. I had them put it at the end where there's a power strip, but I told them to save a bowl for me. He makes the best chili around," she told Lisa, who twisted in her seat and glanced at him over her shoulder.

"Was I supposed to bring a dish?"

"No. You're my date." Something his whole family would know about now. Darcy was a sweetheart, but she told everything—every minute, irrelevant detail—to his brother, Glen, as if she were a sportscaster relaying a play-by-play. Usually all in one sentence. Regardless of their audience. "So maybe you can get those tickets for us before the food starts to get cold?"

Unabashed, his niece took his twenty-dollar bill and gave him two red tickets. "Want to enter the 50/50 drawing?"

"Sure." He handed over a ten. "Give me an arm's worth."

While she pulled a strip of blue tickets from a roll and split them down the middle, he hung his jacket on a rack in the corner.

"Can I take your coat, Lisa?"

She unsnapped the buttons on her quilted parka and pulled her arms free of the sleeves, revealing a whole deck of cards fanning out from the collar of her white T-shirt. A black tutu around her middle topped red-and-black-striped leggings. Shiny black booties with red laces decorated her small feet. She kept her black knit gloves on, and for the first time he noticed the four suits embroidered on the fingertips.

Bending close, he took in the red diamond dangling from one ear while a black spade hung from the other. "You're the Queen of Hearts?"

"Got it in one."

As he hung her coat, he wondered again how it was they hadn't met before. She was attractive, but more importantly, she was interesting.

"So do you know how to play kitty whist?"

"Not a clue."

The only reason he didn't laugh at her saucy wink was because Darcy held out his 50/50 tickets. He stuffed them into his pocket and wheeled Lisa through the open double doors into the main room.

In front of the stage, a long table groaned beneath the weight of assorted pans and crockpots. Steam rising from several dishes warmed the atmosphere with delicious smells and fogged up the long windows. Friendly conversation from red-checkered tables hummed on the airwaves.

"Full house," he noted, nodding to a couple who waved and a man who made eye contact. "Which end would you like to sit on?"

"Most people don't think of that," she said, surprise in her voice. "You know, the fact that I can't simply slide into a space where a regular chair would fit without banging my knees. Or having to sit so far away the food falls in my lap. Do you know someone else in a wheelchair?"

"My wife used one before she died."

The comment demanded explanation, but before he could say more, a young voice from a table on their left shouted, "Hey, Slick, come sit with us!"

Preston Allen stood up in his chair, skinny arms pinwheeling in the air to get his attention.

Belatedly realizing this date wasn't going to allow them even the smallest amount of privacy, he asked Lisa, "That okay with you?"

"Sure."

Gabe and his son moved down one seat, leaving a space open for him to sit beside her.

"Hey! I wanted to sit next to Slick," Preston complained.

"Tell you what," his father said, "you go get a place setting for Lisa, and I'll switch with you when you get back."

The boy was off at top speed. They laughed at his exuberance and the pride he displayed when he reached the picnic basket on the stage and turned, holding up a rolled paper placemat in one hand and a paper napkin around plastic utensils in the other. By the time he dodged adults and returned to their table, Gabe had moved over to make room for him.

"There you go, Lisa."

"Thanks, buddy."

Roger noticed the familiarity between them when she squeezed the boy's shoulder. "I take it you two have met?"

"He comes to the town hall once in a while."

"And drives everyone crazy with questions," Gabe added. "Lisa entertains him when she's there."

"Maisie doesn't like me being in the office. Lisa plays dots with me."

"Dots?"

"Shall we show him, buddy?"

At the boy's nod, she retrieved a pen from the purse slung over the back of her wheelchair while Preston flipped over his paper placemat and slid it across the table to her.

The six-year-old would have to lean over his lap to play any game with her. Accepting their date would have zero intimacy, he said, "Wanna switch with me?"

Preston was up before he finished speaking.

"What are you going to be for Halloween?" Lisa asked while they switched seats. She made circles on the paper at set intervals until a row appeared.

"A Jedi warrior."

"Very cool." She completed another row perfectly aligned with the first. "Make sure you come to my house. I live at Somerset Place on the hill below the hospital."

"But how will I know which one is yours?"

Half the placemat was covered with a grid of dots. Lisa handed him the pen, and he drew the first connecting line between two circles.

"No one else has a giant-sized pumpkin patch covering their front lawn and scarecrows lining their walkway."

"I think I need to see this for myself," Roger said, a feeble attempt to reclaim his date's attention from a first grader.

"As long as you come in costume."

Her smile invited him into the conversation, but Preston wasn't to be ignored. "Lisa, what are you going to be?"

"It's a surprise." She took the pen from him and made a connecting line on the placemat. "You'll have to wait until tomorrow to find out."

Roger chuckled at the boy's crestfallen expression. "Go ahead, torture the poor kid."

The sudden clang of a cowbell drew their attention to the center of the room.

"Hear ye, hear ye!" Dougie Lucas shouted, hitching his thumbs under blue snowflake suspenders. The bell dangling from his index finger shone beneath the chandelier as brightly as the crown of his bald head. "Place is full, and if we don't get this shindig started, the food will dry up in the crockpots. We're going to start on the odd side tonight, then switch to evens, but in reverse since the front people always go first. Nine, then ten. Everybody got it?"

There were nods and murmurs of assent but no movement.

"Well, whadya waitin' for?"

Table nine was still slow getting started. Only a few of the diners had risen from their seats when a sudden cacophony of beeps and tones filled the room.

Chief Price got to her feet immediately. Man after man, and some women, too, checked pagers on their belts.

"Car accident on 114A," Dougie announced.

"Don't eat all the food while we're gone."

A good quarter of the diners hurried out of the hall after the chief.

****

"Way to clear a room," Lisa said with awe.

"Pretty much the whole volunteer fire department comes to these dinners."

"I hope everyone is okay."

A stout woman by the front table stood up and took over for their absent host. "Better not let the food go to waste. Table nine, you're up!"

They were at table five. She and Preston finished their game before their turn, but when she would have put her pen away, Roger snagged it from her hand and flipped his placemat over.

"Draw me!" Preston begged.

What was this?

With just a few strokes of the pen in his blunt-tipped fingers, he made a caricature of the boy standing at the table waving his arms.

"Wow." Even for an impromptu drawing, his talent was clear.

"Do Lisa."

"Not this time. It's our turn to get food."

He walked alongside her to the tables where he explained what each pot held or tilted it for her inspection. Since she couldn't see inside the dishes beyond those at the edge, she appreciated this further proof of his considerate nature.

"Just tossed salad and a small bowl of your chili for me," she chose despite the variety of foods offered.

"Are you on a diet?"

"Always."

His raised eyebrows silently asked for explanation.

"Obesity can be a problem for people like me. You're able-bodied, so you don't have to worry about it the same way." And what a body it was. Seeing him from the other side of the town clerk's window in his barn coat hadn't prepared her for what lay beneath. His belted jeans revealed a trim middle above long legs. The plaid shirt complemented wide shoulders and a lean spine. He wasn't skinny, just fit in the way only a working man could be.

She admired his form while he filled her plate and escorted her back to their table.

"Coffee, tea, water, or juice?" a teenage girl with two metal pitchers offered almost as soon as they were seated.

"Milk."

"Jinx," Lisa said because they had both given the same reply at the same time.

"Did you grow up on a dairy farm, too?"

"Nope. I have milk at lunch and dinner. Good for the bones, you know. But I can't start the day without my morning coffee."

"Same here."

"My friend told me you're a farmer. What time is your first cup of the day?"

"Five o'clock. Been checking up on me, have you?"

Her cheeks warmed, but he didn't make her wallow in the moment.

"I'm flattered. Though it seems you're one up on me. What do you do for a living when you're not at the town hall?"

"I'm the human resources director at the hospital."

"Ah."

She liked his non-answer. "Most people seem surprised when I tell them that. Like it's a big deal for someone in a wheelchair to make it to a position that high up, or like they're surprised I work at all."

"I didn't think you sat around a pumpkin patch all day."

The twinkle in his blue eyes made her tummy flutter. He seemed like such a good, solid man. And truly interested in her, or at least giving that impression. Did that mean this might not be a one-time thing, and he'd want to see her again? Maybe she needed to borrow one of Jonnie's aversion-therapy wristbands and snap it just to wake herself up, because she only met guys like him in her dreams.

He accepted a basket of rolls from Gabe, took one for himself and one for Preston before offering them to her. "What time does an HR person have her first cup of coffee in the morning?"

She chose one, and he passed the basket across the table to the next person down the line from her, three seats away now that the first responders had left.

"Five o'clock."

"I think I'm seeing a pattern here."

"You started it."

He grinned, and she clutched her paper cup to resist wiping the thin line of milk from his upper lip. When he licked it away, she was almost disappointed until he spread butter on his roll, and she got to watch those square, capable hands at work. How could hands be sexy?

"Early to bed and early to rise?"

Pulling her wayward thoughts from that visual

feast, she rejoined the thread of conversation. "Both. I do sixty to ninety minutes of exercises each morning. If I don't get a good night's sleep, they're harder to do and not as effective as they should be."

Preston, who had been remarkably quiet so far, suddenly scrambled up in his chair and waved his arms like he had done earlier. "Over here!"

Following his gaze, she saw Darcy approaching with a plate of food in one hand and a fistful of 50/50 tickets in the other.

"Can I join you?"

"Sure thing, pumpkin." Roger pointed to one of the vacant seats across the table.

Could he see how much she adored him? Lisa had never had any uncles in her life, but if she had, she would have wanted one like him—patient and teasing yet humoring her every word.

"I'll be quick." Darcy put her plate down, unstrapped the bulging cash belt from her waist, and put it on the table before plonking herself in a chair with a sigh. "I still have more to sell."

"I can help!" Preston volunteered.

"Only if you eat your vegetables."

"You sound just like Mémère."

The teenager beamed at Roger. "That's the nicest thing anyone ever said to me."

They talked about the band and chorus trip to her grandmother's native Quebec, high school in general, and Darcy's plans after graduation. It kept Lisa from staring at Roger through the meal. Instead of looking into his blue eyes, she listened to the girl with the matching pair while she rambled excitedly about becoming a teacher and living right here in Somerset.

The best place on earth, she said. "So much better than New York, where I used to live, or California. That's where my mother lives now."

Preston managed to break into the animated monologue long enough to share his preferred Halloween candy list, and by the time they made a second trip to the food table for dessert, the volunteer firefighters and EMTs started trickling in.

"Black ice," Snowflake Suspenders reported, his name in her mind since she hadn't been introduced to him yet. "Weatherbee kid went into a slide by the bridge and stopped himself on a telephone pole."

Around the room several diners gasped.

The man held both hands up, palms out in a reassuring gesture. "Don't worry, he'll be fine. Just got a concussion and a broken arm. I'm sure all the girls will be lining up on Monday to sign his cast."

"Ugh." Darcy groaned. "He's already got a big enough head."

"He *is* cute," Lisa conceded and, when Darcy, Gabe, and Roger all looked at her, added, "He does the yard work and odd jobs at Somerset Place. In fact, he's supposed to pick up the pumpkins for me tomorrow and help me with decorations before the trick-or-treaters come." She didn't want to seem selfish, but this would put a wrench in her plans. "Looks like I'll have to figure something else out."

"You can't *not* have your pumpkin patch!" Darcy wailed.

"I can help you out," Roger volunteered.

She didn't know if it was to see her again or to keep his niece from having a meltdown, so she felt obligated to object.

He easily overrode her arguments. "My youngest son, Bryce, is home from college for the weekend. I'll bring him with me. Where do you get the pumpkins?"

"I don't know. Paul just gets them for me, and the next day he takes them away."

"They must come from Crawfords'," Gabe said, explaining, "my neighbors."

"That would make sense." Roger grabbed Darcy's cellphone from the table, a twinkle in his eye Lisa didn't understand when he asked, "Do you want me to give them a ring?"

"On a Saturday night?"

"Right." Rocking back in his chair, he called across the room to table six, "Hey, Buddy, is the Weatherbee kid supposed to pick up a load of pumpkins from you tomorrow morning?"

"Sure is," a gray-haired man replied, leaning away from his table to converse across the expanse of hardwood floor between them.

"I'll be over to get them instead. Ten o'clock sound okay?"

"You got it."

Dropping the front legs of his chair down onto the floor, Roger smiled at what must have been a bemused expression on her face. "Buddy Crawford says I can get them at ten. Does that work for you?"

"Perfect."

Chapter Three

"I've found the perfect guy," she almost squealed into the phone the next morning.

"You couldn't have," Jonnie fired back. "I'm married to him."

"Okay," Lisa conceded, because her best friend and David were as near matched as any couple she had ever seen, "but I've found the perfect one for me."

"Give me all the details."

Now that she had her chance, she wasn't sure she could explain it. Which made her first comment wildly inaccurate. "He's nice."

"Good start."

"No, I mean, he's nice to everyone. Nice to me. He notices things other people don't when they're with me, like how high up something is or that I might have trouble opening the bathroom door and closing it behind me when I'm in my wheelchair."

"Thoughtful. I like it."

"He's also patient. I've never played kitty whist before, and I had no idea what I was doing. People take their cards seriously! The first time I messed up, I thought Ardell was going to jump across the table and strangle me. She was my partner. But he just explained what I should have done differently and told Ardell the Earth hadn't stopped spinning on its axis."

"What's his name?"

"What?"

"Have you forgotten his name already? I mean, *I* know what it is, but you say *him* and *he*, and you haven't used his name. At this point in our relationship, I was saying, *David this* and *David that*, so I owe you a few."

"Oh." She knew it, of course, but that was the one concern she had about him. Why did they call him Slick? Was he known for being a flirt? For being lucky with women? She tried not to let it bother her, yet it kept a little part of her from diving in the way she wanted to. "Roger. It's a good name, right?"

"Solid."

"That's what I thought, too."

"So when are you seeing him again?"

"Today. The boy who normally puts out my pumpkin patch broke his arm. Roger and his son are coming to do it for me. Which reminds me, I'd better get moving. I want to bake some muffins before they get here, and I don't have a lot of time."

"You mean you're not going to church?" Mock horror laced the question. "It's Sunday!"

"I guess I'll just have to grovel to the minister and do penance for the rest of my life."

They ended the call, and Lisa mixed a batch of batter, layered it with streusel in muffin tins, and popped them into the oven. Roger had said he liked coffee, so she hoped that meant coffee cake as well.

She'd find out soon enough.

Now it was time to get ready.

The people who'd owned the house before her were elderly. Because of this, the bathroom was set up for someone like herself in terms of turnaround space, toilet height, and a shower level with the floor so she could wheel or walk in without falling over a lip. The only thing they didn't get right was the mirror. She could do her mascara with it, but it was too high up on the wall for her to see the rest of her face from her wheelchair, and lowering it wasn't an option because then it would be sitting in the sink basin.

So she was standing, dusting her cheeks with bronzer, when a loud meow echoed off the porcelain fixtures. Mischief poked his feline head around the door as if inspecting the room for potential threats. Apparently deciding the coast was clear, he scratched his chin and neck against the doorframe before padding over to her side.

"Nice of you to join me," she murmured. Some days he slept for hours; some days he didn't. This was the first she had seen of him since leaving yesterday morning.

Not to be ignored now, he forced his way between her feet and rubbed against her ankles. Wrapped his long tail around one shin while simultaneously headbutting the back of her knee. His routine greeting. Only when he had done the same thing on the opposite side did he come around and stand in front of her, tip his head back, and let out a plaintive yowl.

"Come here, you big baby."

Scooping him up in her arms, she snuggled his warm marmalade body. A satisfied purr rumbled out of him. He nuzzled the side of her neck and rolled around in her embrace, basking in every stroke of his fur, every nonsense word of affection she gave him.

That didn't last long. About sixty seconds after begging for her attention, he batted her naked earlobe with one paw and jumped from her shoulder to the toilet seat. After stretching one front paw and the opposite back paw until it looked like his spine would crack, he rolled into a boneless ball on the fuzzy lid cover and closed his eyes.

"Typical cat."

Returning to her makeup, she finished just in time to take the muffins from the oven. Warm butter, vanilla, and brown sugar perfumed the air as they cooled on a rack. She was restocking the coffee carousel when her phone buzzed. Hazel again. Hitting the speaker button, she greeted her sister without much enthusiasm, because she should have called her back the day before and was probably in for a lecture about it. "Hello."

"Happy birthday."

"Thanks." It was as if the stars had aligned thirty-nine years ago, because what could be more perfect than being born on a day when she got to dress as wildly as she wanted to and gorge on sugar?

"I have a card for you. Do you want me to bring it to church?"

Guilt all but strangled her vocal cords. "I'm playing hooky today."

"Oh." Was that disappointment or censure coming through the phone? Hard to tell. "Well, I guess you deserve a day off once in a while. I can bring it over after the service."

"Sounds good."

"All right. Well, I guess I'll see you then."

Awkward. They never really talked to one another the way other sisters did. Hazel was almost four years younger and burdened with having been born able-bodied while Lisa was not. Hazel took her responsibilities as her sister's keeper so seriously they could never just relax and have fun.

Shaking off the conversation, she finished loading the carousel, then went into her room to get dressed for the day.

Her enormous walk-in closet was lined with jewelry and scarves and every accessory she could possibly need for any occasion. Some days she only used her manicure and earrings to celebrate the season. Other days, like today, she went all in.

Below a bustier top, the handkerchief hemline of her black dress fell in ragged beauty over her thighs. The first time she wore it, those ends had curled up when she sat, so she'd added sparkling gems to the points to weigh them down and keep them flat. It worked better than an iron and added even more holiday spirit to her attire.

Pumpkin earrings. Witch's hat. Black booties with little black cats on the top. Mischief loved those. When she laced them up over black-and-orange-striped tights, he sauntered into the room and rubbed back and forth against the plush little accoutrements as if they were stuffed with catnip, leaving stray hairs behind on the cats, the shoes, and the stockings.

"At least we're color coordinated."

He didn't even purr a response, already disappearing into the other room.

"That means you guys are safe," she said to the hideous and beautiful things lining her black satin cape—dead rats, bats, snakes, and howling cats mixed with more sparkling gems.

The doorbell rang. Her nerves went haywire.

Too jumpy even to sit in her wheelchair, she slid

on her forearm crutches and walked on trembling legs to answer.

"Happy birthday!"

Relief had her wilting on the spot. "It's just you."

"Don't get too excited." Jonnie strolled into the open-concept room with a dark-haired, dark-skinned baby in her arms and three little boys trailing behind her. Like the Pied Piper, only she was a Nordic goddess, and the boys were her adopted sons. "I came to spy."

"What?"

"You know, check out this farmer and make sure he's good enough for you."

"You didn't!"

"No. Just pulling your leg. We brought you a surprise."

"Oh, goody." Her love of surprises was no secret. "Should I sit down for this?"

"Whatever floats your boat." Turning to the oldest boys, she spoke in a dramatic stage whisper, "Which present should we give her first?"

"The card," five-year-old Elijah whispered back, then clapped his hand over his mouth as if realizing he might have spilled the beans.

"I love cards," Lisa admitted with a wink to reassure him. Elijah had lived in foster care apart from his younger brothers for several years, and he was still a little nervous in his new home. "But I do think I should sit down to open it, don't you?"

They followed her to the table before the windows where Jonnie claimed one chair with Josiah on her lap while Malachi and Gideon scrambled up into the other two, and Elijah leaned over Lisa's shoulder. His dark eyes shone with excitement when he handed the card to her.

The doorbell chimed again.

Giving Jonnie one terrified, *I'm so excited I might scream* look, she shouted, "Come in!"

Not how she wanted to greet Roger, but given her other company, that's what he got.

He stepped through the door, and her heart thumped once, more like a slow rollover in her chest, reminding her to breathe.

"Good morning." He removed his cap, silver streaks in his thick brown hair catching the morning light, eyes crinkling with his smile. "Lisa, this is my youngest son, Bryce. Bryce, Miss Lisa Kirkpatrick, or as Darcy calls her, the *Halloween Lady*."

She hadn't even noticed the stocky young man behind him. A sure sign of nervous excitement, because he was well over six feet tall if the way he ducked to avoid her overhead light was any indication, and that was after he took off his hat.

"Nice to meet you, ma'am."

"You, too, and thank you for coming. This is Jonnie Wang. Roger, I think you may have met before?"

"That would be correct."

They shared a handshake, and as much as she loved her gorgeous friend, she was pleased to see not one spark of interest on his face.

His voice was merely cordial when he said, "You're the town marketing consultant, right?"

"That's me."

"And who are your little visitors?" His question was directed to Lisa.

"These are Jonnie's boys. That's Josiah." She pointed to the roly-poly baby who only glanced up briefly at the sound of his name, engrossed in playing with his mother's hair. He grabbed a platinum swath between his fat little hands and watched it slide through his fingers only to do it all over again.

The middle boys were eager for attention, though in different ways.

"This is Gideon." She motioned to the little boy whose soulful dark eyes tracked Roger from the moment he entered the house. "And this one is Malachi."

"I'm four," he announced, not a shy bone in his wriggly little body.

"Is that all?" Mock suspicion colored Roger's voice. "You look at least six to me."

"Nope. Elijah's not even six!"

Wanting to commend him for flattering the boy, instead she continued, "These are my very special friends"—she put her arm around the boy at her side— "and this is my new special friend, Elijah."

"Seems like you've got plenty of manpower. Maybe you don't need our help after all?"

"It's her birthday!" Malachi crowed. "We brought her presents!"

Heat crept into Lisa's cheeks though she didn't know why.

"We don't want to interrupt anything."

"No, it's okay. Please come in. I made muffins." She motioned to the golden bells cooling on the counter. "Coffee cakes because you like coffee. Do you want one?"

At his nod, Jonnie stood and wrapped Josiah

around her hip. "I'll get it. You'd better open your card before the boys burst."

****

Roger moved out of her way and leaned against the kitchen island, Bryce beside him. He'd rather watch Lisa open her gifts anyway.

She made a project of it. First sliding one black-lacquered fingernail beneath the bright-pink envelope flap as if it held great treasure, then carefully withdrawing a black velvet card smothered in pink gel writing.

"Did you make this?" she asked Elijah.

He giggled and nodded, his tongue poking out through a gap between his teeth.

"Do you want to read it to me?"

Color suffused his light-brown skin, almost blending with the freckles on his upturned nose. He nodded once, his timid expression disappearing when Lisa squeezed his shoulders and held the card up for him to see.

Peering at the words as if he had forgotten them, he read slowly, "Happy birthday. Thirty-nine." Head swiveling around the room, he explained to her and everyone present, "Because that's how old you are." Gaining confidence, he added, "Look. There's more."

Slowly she opened the black velvet card. Peeking between the folds while Elijah bit his lip and Malachi rocked his upper body on the table with excitement. Gideon stood up in his chair and leaned halfway across the table on his elbows for a better look. They probably all knew what was inside, but their excitement grew when she unfolded the accordion-style card.

"Dimes!" She spread the card open, revealing

silver coins taped in crooked lines across the black velvet. "Look at them all!"

"Thirty-nine of them!" Malachi's glee was so contagious Roger found himself chuckling. Beside him Bryce smiled around a mouthful of coffee cake muffin. Belatedly Roger took a bite of his own and moaned with appreciation.

"But why dimes? Why not pennies?" Lisa asked.

"Jonnie says some friends are a dime a dozen, but you're worth your weight in gold." Elijah shrugged, obviously having no idea what she meant. "I didn't have any gold."

Lisa squeezed the boy close to her side. "I think that is the nicest surprise anyone has ever given me."

"There's more," Malachi announced. "Jonnie, can I get it?"

"Sure can." His mother passed cups of coffee to Roger and Bryce, put out cream and sugar, then resumed her seat at the table.

Malachi dug into a diaper bag hanging over her chair and emerged with a wrapped gift. When Lisa half turned in her seat to admire it, Roger noticed the creatures on the inside of her witch's cape and the marmalade cat sprawled bonelessly over one of her feet.

"Is that thing a decoration, or is it real?"

She nudged the animal with her toe, and his whiskers twitched, but otherwise he didn't move. "This here is Mischief. Most of the time he hides when I have company, but he's staked a claim on the other cats." She wiggled her free foot, revealing the stuffed creature on the bootie.

Malachi slid a gift across the table. "I picked out

the paper."

It sparkled like fireworks on the Fourth of July, streaks of brilliant color topped by a multicolored bow. "I wonder if that thing glows in the dark," Roger mused.

"Good question. Maybe I should just put it in my closet and find out later tonight?"

"No! Open it!"

Winking conspiratorially at the adults in the room, she said, "Okaaay. If you insist."

She was slow about it. First the bow was completely untied, not just released. Then she stretched the ribbons out on the table, smoothing them with her hands until they were a collection of neat and colorful lines. She peeled back the tape but with one fingernail, carefully keeping the paper intact as if saving it to use again later.

"Do you need help?" Malachi demanded, his four-year-old's store of patience gone.

"I think I might." She sighed as if unwrapping the gift had exhausted her. "Maybe you and Gideon can give me a hand?"

Eagerly the younger boys crawled up onto the table and across the surface to her side while their mother slid a floral centerpiece out of the way just in time to avoid a collision.

Lisa didn't bat an eyelash. Beside him Bryce chuckled. So he wasn't the only one who appreciated her going with the flow. Just like last night. In the first hand of the opening game, she'd made an overly cautious bid, and Ardell had given the kitty away. Lisa had six cards in one suit with an ace high, the ace and all face cards in another suit. Together they would have taken almost every trick if Ardell had kept the kitty.

Lisa heard about it.

Another woman might have argued back. Or cried at the verbal abuse she got over a game of cards. Instead, she looked the selectwoman in the eye on the next round and said, "Five." She had a shit hand, but the other pair gave her the kitty, and by carefully discarding and watching what everyone played, she managed to take six tricks, putting their team up before eventually winning the game.

Despite being a quick study, she'd still taken home the booby prize, a pair of black plastic glasses with rainbow-striped eyeballs that popped out like a slinky. He could still hear her throaty laugh when she'd pulled them from the bag.

And there it was again. Only this time it was over a real gift. A ceramic cheetah on a wooden pedestal with a brass turn knob. "Play it!" the boys demanded.

She cranked the knob a few times and let it go. "Wild Thing" by the Troggs filled the room.

"Because you love loud rock music," Malachi explained.

"The louder the better!"

She belted out the lyrics. Malachi tried to sing along, repeating each line after her in a high-pitched echo. Gideon wriggled his body on the table in a parody of dance, but he had rhythm. Josiah ignored them all, and poor Elijah looked scared out of his wits until Lisa pulled him in close for a hug and kiss.

The song ended. Dislodging the cat from her foot, she stood and folded the colorful wrapping paper into a makeshift bag, then filled it with four muffins from the cooling rack.

"These are for later," she cautioned, pressing them into Elijah's hands.

"What do you say?" Jonnie reminded him.

"Thank you, Lisa."

"You're welcome, buddy."

Jonnie handed her a gift certificate to The Gables. "From David and me. Dinner for you and a friend, any time except a Saturday night." Standing, she slung the diaper bag over her shoulder and adjusted the youngest boy at her hip. "Now I think we've kept you from your decorating long enough." She took Elijah's hand on her way past the table. "Time to go, kiddos."

"But we want to help," Malachi objected, not moving. Beside him Gideon bobbed his head in agreement.

"You need lunch and a nap first."

"I don't need no stupid nap."

"If you don't mind Jonnie, I won't save any candy for you."

The boy wasn't old enough to recognize the teasing glint in Lisa's eye. His mouth gaped open at the empty threat. When her countenance remained serious, he snapped his jaw shut with determination and marched across the room to join his mother, his little brother trailing behind.

Lisa stood and slid her arms into aluminum crutches with forearm grips. Grinning at Roger and Bryce, she followed her company.

"We'll be back," a disgruntled Malachi promised.

"I should hope so."

Roger stepped forward and opened the door for them. "Here, let us give you a hand."

With attention from him and Bryce, Malachi

recovered his good humor. The others followed his lead, all chattering with Lisa until their mother got behind the wheel and the last door closed.

Little hands waved from the car windows all the way to the end of the driveway.

"Cute kids," Bryce remarked. Then he read Lisa's vanity plates, "SBBAB. Sounds European." He cocked his head to the side as if that would help him decipher the meaning.

"I don't think you'll figure it out," she warned him. "You can only have five characters on a Vermont handicap plate, so I had to drop the E from the end."

"S-B-B-A-B-E. Nope. Still don't get it." Shrugging, he went to the back of the pickup truck and pulled down the tailgate.

Roger could tell from her impish smile she wanted him to guess what the letters stood for, but he was as clueless as his son. "I give."

"Spina bifida babe."

A laugh spilled out of him. "In your face."

"Hey, I make no apologies for who I am, and I don't like being ignored."

"There's no reason why you should be." Could the woman be any more intriguing? She was sweet but full of sass, as frank as they came, not to mention easy on the eyes.

Bryce approached with an armload of pumpkins, reminding him they weren't just here for a visit. "Ready when you are, Ms. Kirkpatrick."

"Well, we'd better get started if I'm going to be ready for the trick-or-treaters."

Half an hour later they had pumpkins strewn across the lawn amid fallen maple leaves. Scarecrows on wooden stakes marched up the side of the driveway while others were interspersed among the orange fruit.

"Perfect." Lisa clasped her hands in front of her, forearm crutches dangling wildly in the air, her face lit with satisfaction. "This is absolutely perfect. Thank you both, so much."

"You're welcome." Roger closed the tailgate of his pickup truck, turning at the sound of an approaching vehicle.

"I wonder who that could be?" Squinting against the sun reflecting off the truck windshield, Lisa raised her hand to shade her eyes. "It looks like Paul's mother's car, but I already talked to him this morning and told him to stay home and rest."

"Wrong color." Dottie Weatherbee was his neighbor, so he knew it wasn't her car.

The station wagon stopped beside his truck. An attractive woman with straight brown hair stepped out of the vehicle and came around the hood to where he stood with Lisa, Bryce, and her marmalade cat.

"Hello." Her greeting was polite but held a question. Who were they, and what were they doing there?

"Hazel." The lack of inflection in Lisa's voice was a surprise. It wasn't unfriendly, per se, but neither was it welcoming. More like she was saying *left* in response to someone asking which arm she wanted to get a shot in. Stating a preference without any enthusiasm.

The woman extended an envelope to her. Blue-gray, as demure as the navy pullover sweater and slacks she wore, in direct contrast to Lisa's holiday attire. "Happy birthday."

"Thank you."

Roger noticed a chill in the air for the first time. Had the temperature dropped, or was it because he'd stopped working and his body was cooling down after the mild exertion? Or was it from the uncomfortable silence between the two women?

"Well, I guess we should go," he said into the awkward void.

"Oh! Wait, I'm sorry. This is Roger Plankey and his son Bryce. My sister, Hazel."

Her sister must not have noticed the tension in Lisa's face. She extended her hand in a perfectly normal way and greeted the two of them.

Probably not the best time to ask for a second date. Reluctantly, he repeated, "We really do have to go. Bryce promised Darcy he'd go trick-or-treating with her, so he's got to get ready."

"She's decorating the truck," his son said with an exasperated eye roll much like the cousin in question. "Who decorates a vehicle for Halloween, anyway?"

Lisa's throaty laugh filled the still afternoon. "I knew I liked that girl."

Chapter Four

She liked Roger, too, but when he climbed into the truck with his son and left her in the driveway next to Hazel, he didn't ask for her number. Didn't suggest they meet again. Hadn't said he had a good time with her at the Grange.

So was it the proverbial one-night stand? He was a good guy. Maybe he had followed through on his invitation to dinner and the card party because he had used her to get rid of the reality-show contestant, and backing out after the fact would be rude.

But she really wanted to see him again.

All afternoon, she wondered what to do about it. On the outside she laughed and smiled at the kids with their wonderful costumes, from chain-store movie characters to homemade classics. She let the little ones touch the critters on the inside of her cape, let older ones take selfies with her scarecrows.

When Jonnie brought the boys, she wanted desperately to drag her friend inside and get her advice, but another family pulled in right behind her, so all she could do was smile and spoil her little buddies with double helpings of candy before they were on their way again.

Bryce and Darcy arrived just before the official trick-or-treat time ended at five. Lighted pumpkins bobbed haphazardly from a ladder rack which hadn't been on the truck earlier, and gravestones stood on top of the cab while filmy white ghosts dangled from the open tailgate. Half a dozen teenagers climbed off hay-bale perches inside the bed, illegal seating, but who was she to judge? They spilled onto her driveway in all their good humor and outrageous designs.

"I told you I'd be here," Darcy announced, holding the sides of her square costume open.

"Peanut butter and jelly sandwich?"

"You got it. How do you like the truck?"

"It's perfect." Exactly what she would have done as a teenager. If she'd had a truck. If she'd been allowed out on Halloween. If she'd had friends to ride around with.

The Grim Reaper slid out from behind the wheel, reaching back into the cab for his scythe. "Hi, Ms. Kirkpatrick."

No mistaking that height, even more impressive with the black cowl. "Hello, Bryce."

Cleopatra joined them from the passenger side. "Your place looks great, Ms. Kirkpatrick."

"Chelsea!" Until she spoke, Lisa would have never identified the deli girl from The Common Store. Normally her honey blonde curls were confined to a braid and the only makeup on her face some mascara and lip gloss. Seeing her with kohl-rimmed eyes and black bangs was new. "I didn't recognize you, hon."

"That's the point."

"Trick or treat," the other teens chorused, all holding out a bag or pail to be filled.

"Wait! Can we get a picture with you?" Darcy asked. "I'm on the yearbook committee. We should definitely have a picture for the yearbook."

"Good idea. And doesn't Paul put together the pumpkin patch?" someone asked.

"Not this year," Chelsea answered. "He broke his arm last night."

"No way."

"Yes, way. You didn't hear about it? He hit a pole across from the diner."

They talked about the accident while Lisa scooped candy bars from the big orange bowl in her lap and deposited them into their various containers. Then they posed for several pictures, some with her, some in the pumpkin patch, some in and around the truck, and even one with Mischief who made the mistake of venturing outside only to dart away again as soon as they were through with him.

"Thank you so much." Darcy scanned the images on her digital camera while her friends looked over her shoulder at the small screen. "These are perfect."

"Thank you, Lisa."

"Yes, thank you, Ms. Kirkpatrick."

They clambered back into the truck, only Bryce lagging behind for a moment. "Dad forgot to give you his number," he said once the others were out of earshot, handing her a plain white envelope. "He asked me to give it to you."

"Oh." Was the heat in her cheeks noticeable? "Thank you."

"You bet. He'll come get the pumpkins tomorrow unless you need them gone before?"

"They should survive tonight's frost. But thank you. And thanks again for helping today."

With another "you bet" he got into the truck and drove his merry revelers on to their next destination.

A glance at her watch showed four forty-three on the digital screen. Seventeen minutes left of trick-or-treat time. The steady line of cars that had crawled through the housing development were long gone. Maybe done. Mischief sidled around the corner of the carport post, then raced across the distance between them to leap up into her lap. He wrapped his body around the orange candy bowl and batted the critters lining her cape.

"Curiosity killed the cat, you know," she murmured, not sure which one of them she was talking to, but the envelope in her hand was *so* tempting. "I guess it's a good thing I'm not a cat."

She ripped it open and couldn't help but laugh out loud.

You may be warty, but at least you're not forty was printed on the outside, accompanied by a hand-drawn caricature of a witch. One with a black hat, an ugly wart on her chin, and an orange marmalade cat curled around her neck. Inside it simply said, *Happy Birthday, Lisa. Call for a good time* beside a phone number.

"Do you think he drew it himself?" Jonnie asked when Lisa sent her a screen shot of the card the next day.

"I do." Even though she was sitting in a corner booth in the hospital cafeteria, she whispered because certain sounds echoed off the pipes running along the ceiling. "It's pretty good, right?"

"It's cute. She looks like you."

"You think?"

"Duh. Curly brown hair, hazel green eyes? Yeah, it's definitely you."

"Hmm." Lisa took one last look at the card before

stowing it in her purse.

"So did you call him?"

"Not yet."

"But you're going to?"

"What do I say? Hi, thanks for the card, and did you really want me to use this number?"

"Of course, he did. Why else would he have put it in there?"

"I've never called a guy before." Taking a healthy swallow of milk, she admitted, "I'm nervous."

"Because he's special. You wouldn't be nervous if he was a jerk."

"How do you know?"

"Puh-leeze, the guy came and put out your pumpkins for you. After just one date. And he helped me get the boys into the car. He's a good guy."

"Yeah, he is." No point denying it. "He's coming back today to take care of the pumpkins, too. He could be there now for all I know." Most days she enjoyed the view from her office window, rolling fields falling away to the school. Today she wished it faced the road up from the common instead so she could watch her house and see him at work.

Yesterday she couldn't keep her gaze off him. His defined musculature. The way he moved with an economy of motion, making the work look easy.

"Earth to Lisa?"

"Hmm?" Jonnie must have been talking to her.

"I said you have the perfect excuse for calling him. To say thank you for taking the pumpkins away."

"I do, don't I?"

Despite that rationale, she didn't phone him until she was home seated at her dining room table. Talking a good game with her best friend was one thing; actually dialing his number was something else. She needed the familiarity of her own surroundings to bolster her confidence.

"Somerset Dairy, can I help you?"

"Umm," she stumbled, surprised to hear a female voice on the other end of the call. "Hello. I was looking for Roger Plankey."

"This is the Plankey residence."

Oh. Now what? She had just assumed it was a cellphone number.

"Hello?"

"Sorry. Is Roger there? This is Lisa Kirkpatrick."

"He's out doing chores right now. Do you want to leave a message?"

"Can you just tell him I called?"

"Sure."

Only after she thanked that person and disconnected the call did she realize she hadn't left her phone number. Did he have caller ID? She was so used to a cellphone world she didn't know what people with residential landlines had anymore.

She didn't even have the benefit of Jonnie's counsel this time. Mondays were usually manicure days, or *girl time* as David called them, but the social worker who oversaw their adoption home study was coming for a follow-up visit, and that naturally took precedence over her dating anxiety.

Keyed up and disappointed, she reheated a casserole and took it into her room. Not the one she slept in, but the spare across the hall where she made jewelry. She had a lot of stock ready, but it wouldn't hurt to have more for the Christmas craft-fair season, and when she was in the zone, she didn't think about anything else.

At least that was usually the case. Tonight, bouts of intense concentration and creative mindlessness were broken by episodes of complete preoccupation with one blue-eyed farmer.

He didn't call. She finished working on some little-girl bracelets and turned off the lights. Went through her evening routine, maybe dragging it out a bit just in case her phone rang. Unconsciously reasoning that if the lights were on, he would somehow know she was up, whereas turning them off meant she accepted his silence.

She prayed to God, asking Him to make Roger call, then felt guilty for her selfishness when other people were dealing with real problems in their lives.

Fatigue and practicality finally won out over hope. She locked the doors, refreshed Mischief's water bubbler, and got into bed where she told herself a good time on a date didn't mean anything else, and she was no worse off having gone out with him than she had been before they met Saturday morning.

So mature. So sensible. So depressing.

She rolled onto her side and flipped her cellphone over so she wouldn't have to look at it.

But Tuesday was a new day. After using the elliptical machine and free weights, she showered and updated her manicure. A simple design compared to Jonnie's work, but it complemented her pumpkin earrings and autumn-hued scarf without clashing with her dark-brown sweater and corduroy skirt.

She looked professional. Which she was. Professional, independent, and busy.

So busy she had to set a reminder alarm on her phone for bathroom breaks as she worked through a pile of background checks and reference calls. The next rotation of students shadowing and interning with regular staff began in two weeks, and though she shared a part-time receptionist with the hospital administration, sensitive work fell to her.

Most of her morning was spent inside the glass partition that was her office. Ear to the phone and nose to the grindstone except for bathroom breaks at set intervals.

Average people just went when they needed to. With spina bifida she couldn't always feel the pressure letting her know it was necessary, so from a young age she went every two hours whether she felt the urge or not.

Returning from her third break just before noon, she found Roger sitting in one of the chairs by Karen's empty receptionist desk.

"Oh. Hello." Was she blushing, because she was pretty sure her cheeks were warm, but who could blame her? It wasn't just the surprise of seeing him here in her office. The man was a walking advertisement for a farm journal. From the John Deere cap he politely removed on rising to greet her, to the plaid shirt, jeans, and canvas barn jacket, he was tall and strong and made her feel almost dainty. Parts of her that didn't always fire on all cylinders were now sparking to life.

"Hi, Lisa. Hope I haven't caught you at a bad time?"

As if. Out loud she said, "No. Not at all."

"I got your message but didn't have a number to call, so this seemed like the best way to reach you."

At her nod, he continued, "Tomorrow night the Grange is having a silent movie and slapstick comedy show. I wonder if you'd like to go with me?"

"I've never seen a silent movie, and I have no idea what slapstick means."

He smiled at her blunt statement. "Does that mean you'll be there?"

"With bells on."

Now his smile turned into a full-on grin. "Real bells?"

"I think they might mess with the whole *silent* thing."

"True enough." He settled his hat back into place over his thick dark hair. "It starts at seven, goes for an hour, so you should probably be there fifteen minutes early."

"Okay."

"I'll wait for you at the ramp."

"Sounds good."

"I guess I'll get out of your hair, then, and let you get back to work."

She could have let him go, but after almost forty-eight hours wishing she could see him, she wasn't about to let this opportunity pass by. "Can I treat you to lunch?"

"Lunch?"

"You know, the midday meal? I was just on my way to the cafeteria to get some. Do you have time to join me?"

"I'd love to."

****

Roger hadn't expected her invitation. She seemed surprised by it herself, but he gladly accompanied her down the hall from the administrative wing and through the main lobby to a warren of corridors leading to the cafeteria. She walked without crutches, so he adjusted his step to match her pace while he enjoyed watching her in her element.

She greeted each person they passed, by name if she knew them, and everyone seemed glad to see her. That didn't surprise him. Given what he had seen at the dinner and card party, Lisa liked people, and it showed. She was interested in them, listened when they spoke, and generally did her best to brighten their day.

"Tell me about the bells. The costumes," he suggested when they had purchased their lunch and sat at a table in the center of the room because the booths along the wall were taken. This left them somewhat exposed to others coming and going, so it seemed a safe conversation to have out in the open.

"When I went to middle school, my parents made me use a wheelchair."

"You hadn't used one before?"

She shook her head and took a bite of raw carrot, waving the rest in a circular motion while she chewed and swallowed before speaking again. "My elementary school was not much bigger than this room and the kitchen combined. I didn't use anything when we were inside. Only at recess. But the middle school was big. There I was with hundreds of kids, in a wheelchair, and most of them looked past me. Through me."

"They were rude?"

"No." A small frown pleated her brow. "Not really. I think they'd been taught not to stare, and the alternative to that"—she shrugged—"is to not look at all."

"Hard to make friends, then."

"Right. I took it upon myself to get noticed."

He ate a bite of his sandwich and waited for her to continue, but he could just imagine this spunky woman at that age. If she'd been half as independent and determined as she seemed to be now, she must have been a force to reckon with. "What'd you do?"

"My parents volunteered at a thrift shop. I started going with them, and whenever I saw clothes come in that I could work with, I asked for them. I didn't know how to sew then, so at first I just coordinated pieces or draped them."

"You made a fashion statement," he guessed.

"Hmm." She dipped her grilled chicken in a cup of ranch dressing and ate it before opening a small carton of milk. "You better believe it. My parents didn't know what to think."

Her laugh wasn't the deep-bellied sound from this weekend, but it was still infectious. "Anyway, they didn't have money for real fashion, and I was determined to stand out. I decided every day should be a celebration of color. No one would see me coming into a room and not look. Even if they had to look twice, that was better than being ignored, right?"

"Sure. Why not?"

"Halfway through the year I started family and consumer science class and learned to sew. By spring I was doing more than coordinating and draping pieces. I was cutting them up and remaking them."

"So when did the holiday thing start?"

"I'm not really sure. Maybe after I got over my rebel phase."

"You were a rebel?"

"Sort of." She squeezed her milk carton between her hands until the liquid bubbled up to the top of the triangular opening, but instead of taking a drink, she put it down on the table with a sigh. "No, not really. But I wanted to be."

"What were you rebelling against?"

Her wide eyes drifted to her hands, to her nails painted dark red except for the index fingers decorated to look like flint corn. "Fate."

She spoke at the same time someone came through the swinging kitchen door, and he wasn't sure he heard her. She repeated the answer anyway. "My fate, I guess. Having to schedule everything, never able to be spontaneous, being poor, being stuck in a wheelchair. You know they used to say *wheelchair bound*? It didn't mean anything, people weren't trying to be rude, but it pretty much summed up our limitations, at least in the eyes of the average person. Bound to a wheelchair. The sum total of my life."

"But you said you didn't always use one."

"No." She palmed her milk carton and lifted it to her lips, this time taking a long drink before continuing. "My parents kept me home, away from other kids, until I was in third grade and begged to go to school. Then they would only let me go if I went in a wheelchair. They were afraid I'd get hit or run into by someone playing and not paying any attention. I don't think they realized the chair would keep anyone from playing with me at all. I mean, when we were in the classroom, I was allowed to walk around, and when we were at our desks, I was just another kid in a chair, but out on the field, at recess, I wasn't one of them.

"By the time I was eleven, I tried leaving it at the

entrance to the classroom and walking outside on my own. Of course, the teachers couldn't let me do that because they might get in trouble, so they called my parents, who gave me one of those *stern talks* about how I wasn't like other kids, and they only wanted what was best for me."

"That's normal."

"Right. Normal. Sometimes I hate that word so much."

A couple of people in scrubs passed close by their table, and he let the conversation drop until they had gone.

"Tell me about being normal. And your rebellion."

"I threw tantrums. Went outside in the cold and rain and refused to come in. Wore way too much makeup and dressed like a tramp. Not a nineteen-twenties tramp, you know, but a slut with heavy kohl and too much flesh on display. I locked my bedroom door and blasted rock music so loud the neighbors complained."

"Sounds like a teenager to me."

She smirked at that, but the smile only briefly lit her eyes before they were somber again. "I think I was trying to prove the restrictions didn't apply to me. That the doctors were wrong, my parents were wrong, and I could overcome my physical disability and be normal."

Roger's meal was finished, so he brushed the crumbs from the table into his palm, then dusted them off onto the cardboard serving tray. He crushed his empty milk carton and balled up the plastic wrap from his sandwich.

"Sorry." She sighed, putting the remnants of her own meal on her cardboard tray. "I didn't mean to get all heavy on you."

"It's fine." He collected both trays and took them to the recycling bin at the side of the room, then returned to their table. "Can I walk you back to your office?"

"Sure."

They didn't speak, though Lisa again greeted everyone she met.

The receptionist's desk was still empty when they arrived at her office. Roger closed the frosted door behind them, giving them privacy, so when she turned to face him and presumably thank him for joining her for lunch, he put a finger to her lips.

"Before you send me on my way, can I get your number?"

Her hazel eyes went wide, and she blushed like she expected him to say something else and was embarrassed when he didn't. Maybe she thought her story revealed weakness, but he saw just the opposite— a strong and resilient woman, lacking only someone to appreciate those qualities. So when she scribbled her phone number on a sticky note and handed it to him, he didn't even look at it. Just tucked it inside his billfold, took her by the shoulders, and leaned down so they were eye level. "Can I kiss you, Lisa?"

His voice was a rumble, even to his own ears.

Her long eyelashes flickered once, and she nodded.

He gave her a gentle salute. When he started to pull away, she softened against him, and he returned for more, enjoying the way her soft curls brushed his cheek, and her floral scent filled the space between them.

Finally taking a step back, he said, "Huh. That

surprised me."

"Why?"

"The way you talked, I thought maybe your disability extended to other parts of your body, but those lips of yours? Turns out they're perfectly *normal*."

Chapter Five

Snow was falling on Wednesday afternoon when she left the hospital at four thirty. Light and fluffy, but the forecast called for it to pick up by six o'clock and leave eight to ten inches on the ground before ending sometime in the wee hours of the morning. She had been looking forward to their date like a little kid waited for Christmas day.

When Hazel called to say Wednesday night Bible study had been canceled due to the storm, she was relieved she wouldn't have to make any excuses for not being there. But if Bible study was called off, what chance did a slapstick comedy show have?

So when her phone rang a few minutes after six and Roger's number showed on the screen, she braced herself for the inevitable letdown. "Lisa Kirkpatrick here."

"Hi, Lisa, it's Roger."

"Hello."

"The snow has already started, and it's supposed to get worse right around the time we'd be leaving tonight's show."

"I saw that." Realizing her conversation so far had been stilted, she tacked on, "They're calling it off?"

"What? No. I just thought maybe I should pick you up instead of you meeting me there, if that's okay. I don't want you trying to move your wheelchair through any heavy accumulation."

"Oh." *So* not what she had been expecting. It was Christmas morning again, and her stocking was full. "Well, thank you. That would be great."

"All right, I'll be at your place at quarter to seven."

The snowdrifts were already ankle deep when he arrived, so she left her wheelchair in the living area and waited at the door with her crutches.

Roger looked from her to the inches of snow between her carport and his truck, said, "This won't do," and before she could guess what he had in mind, he bent and scooped her up in his arms, crutches and all.

"You can't do this!"

"Why not?"

"I'm not exactly a lightweight, you know." She worked hard to keep below one thirty on the scale but knew for a fact she had inched above that thanks to Halloween candy.

He tossed her into the air, making her yelp and clutch his shoulders while her crutches flailed wildly around them. "You weigh next to nothing."

She stopped arguing because being in his arms felt especially nice after preparing herself for a cancellation just two hours ago. Letting him deposit her into his truck was also easier than it would have been for her to climb in since the vehicle sat several inches above the ground.

"Is this a monster truck?" she asked above the rumble of the diesel engine while he stowed her crutches behind the bench seat.

"No, just a work rig." Leaning into the interior, he kissed her on the cheek. "Nice to see you again."

Lisa's pulse tripped. He made her feel about fourteen years old. Back when falling in love with a boy meant dreaming about him but never actually talking to him. The idea of love, rather than any real connection between them, constituted love at that age.

Whoa! Why was she even thinking about that four-letter word? They had been out on one date, met again twice since then, and she hardly knew the man.

"Don't forget to buckle up," he said as he reversed the truck out of her drive and coasted down the curving boulevard to where it met the main road. Both had been plowed half an hour ago, but already a fresh layer of snow coated the pavement. He shifted his truck into four-wheel drive. "This is shaping up to be quite a storm."

"Yes. Thanks for getting me."

"Didn't want to see the show without you."

She suspected he could find plenty of other people to sit with, but she didn't say that because she wanted to be with him. She also didn't protest when he carried her to the ramp from his truck, supporting her while she got her crutches under her and found her balance again.

Nuzzling her cheek before releasing her, he said, "You smell nice."

"Hey, Slick, stop hogging the walkway," someone called from behind them.

Roger guided her to the side and greeted the newcomer even as they proceeded up the ramp. "How you doing, Dougie?"

"Fair to middling," the other man replied, running his gaze over Lisa from the top of her knit cloche to the bottom of her aluminum crutches.

Now that they were under the light above the

doors, she recognized him even without his snowflake suspenders.

His next words said he remembered her, too. "You were at the card party this weekend, weren't you?"

"I was."

"Well, don't be a stranger. We can always use another pretty face at the tables." He stepped forward and opened the door for the two of them. "See you later, Slick."

"Later, Dougie."

Tonight, Chelsea sat at the table selling tickets.

"Hi, Ms. Kirkpatrick."

"Hi, hon, how's my favorite deli girl?" To Roger she said, "Chelsea makes the best turkey club sandwich at The Common Store. I only get it when she's working."

"Good to know."

The young woman beamed at both of them, her gaze drifting to Roger's hand at Lisa's waist before belatedly greeting him. "Hey, Mr. Plankey. Admission for two?"

"Yes." Roger extracted his wallet from his back pocket and handed over a twenty-dollar bill. When she would have given him a few dollars in change, he said, "Keep it for the scholarship fund."

"Thanks, Mr. Plankey."

"Don't you think it's about time you called me Roger?"

A blush stained her cheeks, and Lisa wondered about it until he added, "With the amount of time you spend at the farm, it seems kind of silly for you to call me mister."

"Okay, Mr.—I mean, Roger." She put the money

into a zipper bag and added a note about the scholarship donation. "Enjoy the show."

"What was that all about?" Lisa asked when he took her elbow and led her into the main room. Rows of folding wooden chairs filled the hall, facing the stage with a center aisle between them. Along the wall long wooden benches held additional guests. He steered her to the right side.

"She and Bryce are seeing one another."

"Is it serious?"

"Seems that way. She goes to college down in Lyndon but as an online student. I think that's about being available when he comes home on break and when he finishes his degree. He's two years older than her, so he'll graduate before she does."

"And does he feel the same way? They seem awfully young."

He shrugged. "I was married at eighteen."

Wow. She remembered eighteen. Finally gaining some freedom with her high school graduation, going to college, and having a roommate for the first time. Dorm parties. Classes. Exams. Hoping to meet someone but ending up with only a handful of disappointing dates that never turned into callbacks from the guys or any desire for them from her.

Roger found an empty spot for them, slid her crutches beneath the bench, and bunched their outerwear up like lumbar pillows against the wall.

"Did you ever regret it?" she asked while settling in.

"Regret what?"

"Getting married at eighteen."

"No." He spread his legs out in front of him,

relaxing his spine against the wall.

"Really? Most people don't know what they want or even who they are at that age."

He shrugged. "Mindy and I started dating in eighth grade. From then on, there was no one else for either one of us and nothing we wanted except to live on the farm together and raise our family there. So, no, I have no regrets. Not a single minute, not a single day."

His answer left her mute. She couldn't imagine that kind of certainty at thirty-nine, let alone as a teenager. Yet she wasn't surprised; it wasn't just his name that was strong and steady.

"Are these seats taken?"

"No." Lisa tucked the edges of her parka closer to her body, giving the couple asking plenty of room. "Please help yourself."

Probably in his sixties, the man was trim and handsome with deep grooves on either side of his mouth, suggesting he smiled often. His partner was tall for a woman and strikingly attractive with gray-streaked dark hair and deep blue eyes.

"You must be Lisa," she said once she was seated.

"I am. Have we met?" No way would she forget that accent, soft and slurred, reminiscent of a rambling summer breeze.

"Lisa, this is my mother, Françoise," Roger explained, "and my father, John."

"Oh." Surprise turned to pleasure because he was the first man to introduce her to his parents, even informally, and his mother already knew her name. "It's nice to meet you both."

"You, too," they chorused, and the overhead lights flickered to indicate the show was about to begin.

"Thank you for asking me," she said when they were in the doorway to her house later that evening, Mischief wrapped around her calves, the truck's running lights shining on them from the driveway. Silence only heavy snow brought held them in a cocoon of white. "I had a good time."

"Me, too. Think you're up for another game of cards this Saturday?"

"Absolutely. I have something to prove to Ardell."

He grinned at her declaration.

"But this time I'll bring a dish, and you can come as my date."

"Deal. Can I pick you up, or do you want to meet there again?"

"You can come and get me."

****

Roger knew by mid-afternoon on Saturday he wouldn't make it to the supper. Fall was calving season, and he had two heifers in labor. Both were healthy, but first births were tricky, and he couldn't leave them unattended. His parents had driven his great uncle down to Lyndon to visit his wife in the rehab center she was in following surgery, and the boys, Bryce and Colin, were at Darcy's first volleyball scrimmage up in Newport. That left only him and one of their employees, Tony, at the farm.

"I'm sorry about this," he told Lisa on the phone. "My sister, Linda, is coming over after the diner closes, and my brother, Glen, is going to give her a hand with the milking if my parents don't get back in time, but that already leaves us understaffed, and they can't milk and look after the heifers, too."

"It's okay. Of course, you need to be there."

He still felt like a heel. "Listen, if my folks and the boys are back and everything's going okay, I'll swing by. If that's all right?"

"Sure. Don't worry about me. You do what you've got to do."

He hung up, not knowing if her responses were genuine or if she was just telling him what she thought he needed to hear. That was the problem with a new relationship, that uncertainty, and he hadn't felt it in years. About a dozen years, in fact, and the couple of women he'd dated back then were not half as interesting as Lisa was.

Nothing he could do about it now, though. He filled a thermos with coffee and headed out to the barn.

The first calf dropped at six o'clock and stumbled to its feet thirty minutes later, just before the kids returned from the game. "I thought you were going to the supper with Lisa." Darcy leaned over the stall fence and eyed the calf with its matted hair and spindly legs.

"Couldn't leave my girls." He rubbed the calf's belly dry with a towel. "Did you win your scrimmage?"

"Twenty-two to twenty-three."

"Close one. How was your game?"

"Two rebounds, three assists, eight points." She lifted her phone and took several pictures of the dam licking the small bovine face, the power of her caress almost knocking the little one over. "Can I help?"

He pointed to a bottle next to the gate. "Grab the iodine tincture for me."

Glen and his children had lived in New York until a couple of years ago, and as much as Darcy had enjoyed farm life on the occasional weekend visit, she'd missed out on a lot of firsts. Taking care of newborn calves was one of them. Her eyes wide with excitement, she passed him the bottle.

"You need to wash your hands."

"Of course." She slid the phone into her pants pocket, pushed up the sleeves of her hoodie, and went to the sink on the other side of the alley. "The boys are helping Pop and Linda finish up with the milking, then they'll be over here."

"Mémère and Papa back yet?"

"No. Linda said they called, and they're going to be late. The rehab center is letting Aunt Carolyn come home tonight."

Until that moment he thought he might be able to get away for a while and see Lisa. At least make his apologies face-to-face. She said it wasn't a problem, but people outside agri-business didn't always understand how much a farmer was tied to his work. He wanted to reassure her that if he had a choice, he'd rather be with her than have his hand inside a cow's uterus, helping it through its first labor.

"What now?" Darcy stood before him like a scrub nurse, hands wet and pink, face bright with anticipation.

"Now we disinfect the navel." He grabbed the teat cup from a shelf outside the pen and handed it to her. "Hold that while I fill it with iodine."

She hooked her index finger beneath the handle and held the clear plastic base with her other hand. "I like Lisa."

Roger filled the cup and smiled at his irrepressible niece. "I like her, too."

"Do you think you'll see her again? I mean, after tonight. Or were you just asking her out because you felt sorry for her, and you're a nice guy?"

"Take the umbilical cord and dip it into the iodine, all the way up to the belly."

She held the cup by the handle and threaded the cord through the wide blue mouth, squeezing the bottle as instructed.

"If I asked her on a date out of pity, that wouldn't make me a very nice guy after all."

A look of relief crossed her young features. Apparently, he'd passed her litmus test.

"What's this for?"

"If the calf is wet and lies down, she can pick up all kinds of bacteria and get sick or even die. We do this after birth, and we'll do it again tomorrow. This tincture dries out the cord and protects against infection."

"Awesome. Now what?"

"Now we need to see if she'll suckle. Calves don't have any immunity without their mother's colostrum. Or, in the case of this little one, colostrum from a mature cow. I've got two quarts thawing on the freezer."

"That's the early milk after birth, right?"

"You been reading up on this stuff?" he teased, but he was impressed as always by her curiosity and intelligence. Maybe it was because he only had sons, but he loved spending time with this girl.

"I've read some. Abby also explained colostrum to me when the twins were born."

He did *not* want to think about his sister-in-law's breasts and newborn calves in the same conversation. Ignoring her comment, he put the teat cup back on the shelf.

"And you gotta admit, Justin and Grace are healthy little kids," she added.

"Cute as hell, too." His brother strolled down the alley to join them.

"Hey, Pop, Uncle Roger let me dip the calf."

Glen hooked his rubber boot on the bottom bar of the calving pen and draped his forearms over the top. At six and a half feet tall, he wasn't even stretching. "Better be careful. He'll make a dairywoman out of you yet."

"You know I'm going to be a teacher."

"That's what you tell me. Need any help?"

"I could use the skid steer to change the bedding." Roger indicated the sand in the pen, dark and wet with afterbirth.

"I'll get it!" Darcy sped down the alley to where a small tractor sat by the doors.

"Any excuse to get behind the wheel," Glen said, affection in his gaze as he watched her hop up onto the seat. Turning back to Roger, he lowered his voice. "That gives us about sixty seconds before she's back, trying to get up in your business. Do you need a break to see this lady you stood up?"

Roger shook his head. "Why am I not even surprised you know about that?"

"The kid's heart is in the right place."

They both turned to watch *the kid* approaching on the tractor.

"Well, if you wouldn't mind?"

For answer, his brother opened the gate and stepped into the pen.

Chapter Six

Lisa was in the middle of making an intricate brooch when her doorbell rang. Odd, because she didn't get company at this hour, so she kept the pin vise in her hand with the cup burr pointing away from her body in case she had to defend herself against a villain.

Instead, Roger stood beneath her outside light.

He removed his hat when she opened the door. Dark swirls of damp hair clung to his skull, and warmth shone from his blue eyes, but she didn't miss the lines of fatigue surrounding them.

She wanted to pull him inside and make him put his feet up. Spoil him with a hot cup of cocoa or something stronger and let him sleep for an hour. Instead, she stood back and simply said, "Come in."

"Is that a weapon?"

"What?" She looked down, having forgotten the pin vise in her hand. "Maybe."

"I'm trembling."

"I think it would take more than this to scare you. But don't worry. The crazy lady isn't lurking around the corner."

"Crazy lady? Oh, right. The reality-show contestant. I haven't seen her since that day at the town offices."

"Good. Then I won't be needing this." She returned the jeweler's tool to her craft room.

Roger followed her to the doorway. "So this is where the magic happens?"

"You got it."

She turned to view the room as he might see it. Plastic tubs stacked with materials, a worktable, and a bright lamp on a flexible neck, her sewing machine in the corner.

"What do you do with the jewelry?"

"I have a table at craft fairs. I'm building up inventory for the Christmas season now."

He fingered a plastic bag with drop earrings. "It looks like Trevor and Amy's spare room in New York. My first son and his fiancée," he explained, "only you have more floor space."

"How did he end up in New York?"

"My brother, Glen, lived and worked there. Trevor always admired him, so when Amy got accepted to NYU grad school, they took off. He was never meant to be a farmer."

Which reminded her of his earlier call. "How is the calf? The mother?"

"Both good. Thanks." He bounced his hat on the tip of one finger. "Glen took over for a few minutes so I could apologize to you in person."

"I told you it was okay."

He shrugged, and she noted the width of his shoulders in the canvas barn jacket. Strong and square, like his hands.

"Maybe I just wanted an excuse to see you again?"

She wasn't sure what to make of that comment. Every part of her wanted to believe he was exactly what he appeared to be—an honest, hard-working, down-to-earth farmer who just happened to be incredibly handsome on top of it. But his nickname kept worrying the back of her mind, preventing her from relaxing the way she wanted to in his company.

"Why do they call you Slick?"

If her question surprised him, he didn't show it. "Been bothering you?"

She shrugged. Of course, it had. In a community where men outnumbered women three to one, she hadn't been asked on a single date since moving here two years ago. Now he'd come into her life and seemed so perfect she kept waiting for the other shoe to drop.

"Earth to Lisa."

She shook her head and brought her glazed eyes into focus. "Sorry, what?"

"I said, has my nickname been worrying you?"

"A little."

"Then come with me tomorrow, and I'll show you how I got it."

She mentally went through her Sunday agenda. Laundry could be put off until Monday afternoon. Groceries on Tuesday. Seeing that he waited for an answer, she said, "My slate's clear. I'm all yours."

"I like the sound of that." Stepping forward, he placed a soft kiss on her eager lips. "Dress warm. And bring a swimsuit. I'll pick you up at ten o'clock."

He said goodbye before she had a chance to process that last sentence. Ten o'clock on a Sunday meant missing church. Again. Hazel wouldn't be happy.

That was an understatement. Her ears were still ringing with echoes of their argument while she sat waiting for him the next morning.

"You're putting him before God?"

"Don't be ridiculous." That had been her sister's emotion talking. They both knew her faith was absolute. Tested and tried multiple times during her thirty-nine years. Taking one Sunday off from church, or two, wouldn't change that.

"What do you really know about this guy, anyway? It seems like he snaps his fingers, and you jump. Okay, not literally," Hazel conceded, "but you just met the man."

"And this is how I'll get to know him." She wanted to add a *duh* to that statement, but her sister wasn't done.

"He's already thrown off your schedule. Does he even know how important routine is for your health? And what's he after, anyway?"

Even though the question was one she grappled with herself, hearing it from her little sister blew the lid off her temper.

"Maybe he likes me!"

Silence. Fraught with emotion, repentance, and concern, it lasted no more than fifteen seconds but seemed to capture years of tension between the two of them. The older sister treated like an invalid. The younger sister laden with responsibility.

"I'm sorry," Hazel had finally said. "It's just that you don't have a lot of experience with men, and I don't want to see you hurt."

The rumble of a truck engine pulled her mind from memories of their argument and into the present. A door slammed. She pulled her coat from a hook on the wall and put it on just before the doorbell rang.

"Come in!"

He brought the cold air with him, and if it had a

scent, it would be clean. Crisp and bright and refreshing, it wiped away the ugly remnants of the phone call with her sister.

"Ready to rock and roll?"

"Always." She pulled a Berber wool hat down over her ears and took matching mittens from her pockets. "Am I dressed okay?"

He inspected her wooly mukluks and the flannel lining the rolled-up cuffs of her pants. "Perfect."

When she wheeled past while he held the door wide, he added, "And I always have a blanket in the truck. We can use it if you get cold."

"Just where are we going? The North Pole?"

"You'll see."

He put rock music on the radio while he drove. For her, she suspected, but for once it didn't soothe her the way it usually did. Loud drums and long guitar solos were nothing but noise today, and they couldn't keep thoughts of her argument with Hazel from creeping back into her head even though she tried to resist them.

"You okay?" Roger finally asked when they had been on 114 South for several minutes and she hadn't said a word.

"Yes." She drew the last consonant out on a sibilant sigh. "Just an argument with Hazel."

"Ah."

He didn't ask for further explanation, but she wanted to talk about it. "She's almost four years younger than I am, and she's worried about me."

"About you or about us?"

"Both, I guess. She's afraid you won't take good care of me."

"Last time I checked, you were a grown woman

capable of taking care of herself."

"Thank you!" She appreciated him crediting her with knowing her own mind, not assuming her disability carried over to other areas of her body.

"My kid sister can be a pain like that, too."

"Oh?"

He signaled to pass a slow-moving plow truck, drove by it, then back into their lane. "When Mindy died, Linda was still a teenager. She tried to make up for our loss, I guess. Suddenly she was playing surrogate mom to the boys, doing our laundry without asking if I needed her help."

"Did you? Need her help, I mean?"

Glancing her way, he shook his head. "No. Maybe for the first few days, but not permanently. I'd already been doing for myself and the boys before we lost Mindy, since she was so sick and unable to get around much. And Maman was there, of course."

"But your sister felt responsible?"

He nodded. "She hasn't stopped since."

Lisa looked out the window at the fat flakes of snow falling on the quiet morning. "Hazel has a *thing* about being my self-appointed guardian. I appreciate her help, really I do, but..." She stopped, not sure how to explain it.

"But she's smothering you."

"Exactly."

He flipped on his blinker as they approached Lyndon, leaving 114 for 122. After making a couple of turns, he brought the truck to a stop before a long, windowless white building with a corrugated tin roof, close enough that she could see the walkway but not the front door. A few other vehicles were scattered around the gravel parking area, and an SUV pulled in behind them. While Roger was taking her wheelchair from the truck bed, she saw two men exit the other vehicle carrying long black bags. Long enough to hold rifles.

"Is this a shooting range?" she asked when he opened the door for her.

"Nope." His boyish grin spoke of his excitement.

Still at sea, she settled into her chair and accepted the folded blanket he handed her before retrieving his own long bag from behind the truck's bench seat.

"You want a push, or you want to do it yourself?"

"I'll do it."

Foolish pride. Her mittens, the warmest hand coverings she owned, didn't have much grip and slid uselessly over the wheels of her chair. "On second thought, I could use some help."

"Gladly." He slung the bag over his shoulder and pushed her around the truck to the walkway. Now she could see the double-door entrance and the red sign above saying *Fenton Chester Arena*. Not a shooting range, then.

"Horseback riding?" What else would be in an arena?

He stopped at the doors and propped one open with his foot so they could go inside. "You don't get out enough."

Cold air tickled her nostrils, carrying a scent like the ocean. Loud noises sporadically rent the silence. Something banging hard against an equally hard form. Swishing sounds drew near, then retreated.

"Figure it out yet?"

Not until he opened the second set of double doors and she saw players warming up on the other side of a plexiglass wall. They sent puck after puck across the ice, and she jerked a little at the loud impact when they hit the wood half walls or the plexiglass above. Players sped past to retrieve them, only to sail the puck in the other direction. "Your nickname means you're fast on the ice?"

"Bingo." He hefted his bag and nodded to a door on their left. "I've got to suit up. Do you want to sit in your chair or have a seat on the bleachers?"

She looked at the shallow rows of wooden benches curving along the concrete apron surrounding the rink. Narrow seats, with limited room. And if the small number of people huddled in their winter coats with steaming travel mugs in hand were anything to go by, her chair would probably be warmer than the alternative. "I'm good here."

"Okay, but if you need anything, and I mean this, just raise your hand. I'll see you."

"I'll be fine."

He checked on her between periods anyway. Got her a cup of hot cocoa and made sure her blanket was tucked around her feet so they wouldn't get cold. She was so excited, her blood pumping just from watching him, she couldn't even feel the temperature around her.

That excitement was bubbling inside her when he swept across the ice on almost silent blades and joined her at the edge of the rink after the play ended.

"Hey, Slick, good game." A burly, bearded man high-fived Roger on his way off the ice.

"You, too, Chase."

Other players stepped over the wooden retaining wall, each exchanging a word or two with Roger as they passed. Behind him a Zamboni machine rolled onto the ice and scraped its way around the perimeter of the rink, a motorized squeegee dropping a sheet of water in its wake.

"So whadya think?"

"I think you earned that nickname. You fly on those skates."

"Hmm."

"And I'm a little jealous. Even when my family eased up on my restrictions, I could never do anything like that. The closest I came is going downhill on a bicycle without using the brakes."

The machine came closer, and Roger stepped out onto the rubber mat beside her. The other players were in the locker room. A few had already left the building.

"You must have to get changed. I can wait for you by the door."

"I have another idea."

Reentering the rink, he talked briefly to the Zamboni operator before returning to her side. "Can you ditch that chair for a few minutes?"

"Sure." The wheel locks were already set. She folded the blanket and handed it to him to hold while she flipped the footrests out of the way and stood, then put the blanket on the seat behind her. "What are we doing?"

He held out a gloved hand, palm up. "Do you trust me?"

An easy question. For answer, she put her own hand in his and followed him onto the ice where he spun around and held her by the waist. "Put your feet on my skates." When she did that, he wrapped one arm around her back and waved the other over his head.

Only then did she notice the Zamboni had stopped

moving. No sooner had she registered that absence of sound than a hard-rock number blasted from the wall-mounted speakers and filled the arena.

"Dance with me."

She didn't have a choice. He pushed off with one foot and she clutched his shoulders, making him laugh.

"I've got you."

Did he ever. She wanted to burrow into his Vermont Catamounts jersey and stay wrapped in green-and-gold polyester for the rest of her life. Absorb the warmth of his flexing muscles and drown in the scent of citrus, cedarwood, and perspiration.

They circled the rink twice. She found his rhythm and learned to follow each movement with her weight.

"You good?"

"I'm wonderful!" she shouted, swaying from side to side with each thrust of his thighs.

His muscles clenched against her own, and he picked up his pace.

The music escalated in speed and volume. When it broke on the bridge, he said, "Let go of my arms."

As soon as she removed her hands, he lifted her into the air by the waist and flipped her around. So fast she barely had time to get nervous before he lowered her feet down onto his skates and pulled her back against his torso.

"Let's try it this way."

His arms wrapped around her. His chin rested on her shoulder, cheek pressed to hers, their warm breaths mingling in a cloud of joy. They had been skating fast before, but now they flew over the ice. She didn't have to anticipate his movements, only keep her limbs loose and let him be her guide.

They ran into the wind. Her snowflake earrings whipped back into her hair. Cold bit into her cheeks. She grasped his wrist with one hand and let the other fall to his hip, holding on at the same time she let go in a way she never had before.

Her scream of pure happiness rose to the rafters.

"That's my gal."

Rough words of high praise against her ear.

A second song came over the speakers, slower than the last but more rhythmical. He zigzagged across the ice. Broader strokes. Deeper bends. She reveled in their synchronized movements. Was flattered by the hard bulge against her backside. Didn't think twice about turning her face up to meet his when his lips brushed her earlobe, then drifted across her cheek to capture her mouth in a long, warm kiss.

He slowed their pace. Curled his larger body around hers and raised his head to gaze into her eyes.

She couldn't look away. There was blue, then there was Roger Plankey blue. It should be a color in the palette of the jewelry stones she pored through when buying materials for a craft fair. It should be a paint choice at the Aubuchon Hardware Store. Really, everyone should have just one glimpse of that light, bright hue.

The music stopped, but her breathing increased in tempo. He coasted toward the opening in the rink, turning his body at the last minute so he bumped into the half wall and protected her from impact.

"I have to change," he said.

"Okay."

Neither one of them moved.

"I'll meet you at the front entrance?"

"Okay."

Smiling, he gave her a quick peck on the cheek, then nuzzled the side of her neck with his chin, the abrasion against her tender skin pulling a response from the center of her body. Her toes curled in an effort to keep her grounded when all she wanted was to lift herself up for more.

With a grimace that was good for her ego, he loosened his hands at her waist and steered her out of the rink onto the rubber mat. "I'll be out in five, ten minutes tops."

That gave her enough time to use the restroom. Because if she wasn't careful, she would have a spontaneous orgasm right there in the ice rink, and with spina bifida, that could prove messy.

"So what did I need a swimsuit for?" she asked once they were on the road again.

"Maybe I just wanted to see what you looked like in one?"

His tone was teasing, but already she knew him better than that and said nothing, waiting for his answer.

"It was cold at the rink. I thought you might enjoy spending some time in the hot tub."

"You have a hot tub?"

"Sounds like that idea appeals to you."

"You noticed?"

"Let me feed you first." He pulled into the only fast-food restaurant in Lyndonville, gave their order to the drive-through attendant, and a few minutes later they were heading north.

They ate quietly. When their meals were no more than balls of paper wrapping stuffed in a trash bag, he hit the search button on the radio. The first station was mostly static, so he hit it again.

"You don't have to play music for me."

"No?"

"I do love rock and roll, but I'd rather talk if that's okay with you."

For answer, he hit the on/off switch. "Anything in particular you want to talk about?"

"Tell me about your family. I've met Bryce, your parents, your brother, and Darcy. Anyone else I'm likely to run into on my way to the hot tub?"

"Maybe my sister, Linda, or my aunt and uncle. Great aunt and uncle, actually, Zeb and Carolyn. They live in a house on the back of the property. It's on the other side of 114, so they actually live in Morgan while the rest of us are in Somerset."

"And do they work on the farm with you?"

"Everybody does. It takes a lot of hands, but that also means we can have a night off once in a while. You know, for taking a pretty lady to a card party or to a show at the Grange."

They chatted some more about dairy farming, the state of agriculture in Vermont, and his family. She learned his brother, Glen, was divorced from Colin and Darcy's mother but remarried David Wang's sister, and they had one-year-old twins. Linda was single at thirty-something—he thought she was thirty-five, maybe thirty-six, but he wasn't sure because of when her birthday fell—and he didn't know if she would ever find someone to spend her life with.

"She's a good person, but she's pretty strong willed. I don't know if there's anyone who'll put up with that."

"You have a problem with strong-willed women?"

"No. But you have to give once in a while, too. She thinks she's happiest when she's bossing someone around and they're agreeing with her."

"You don't think so?"

"Hell, no. She needs someone who will stand toe-to-toe with her. Put up some resistance. Otherwise, she's like a little general with no checks and balances."

Chapter Seven

A few minutes later he veered off 114 to refuel the truck at a diesel station north of Island Pond. This brought them into Somerset from the southeast, where he made almost a complete circle around the town common before taking the last right west onto 114A.

The road swooped up and down like a roller coaster. Up past Dottie Weatherbee's tree farm, down by the town sheds and rail yard, up and down again until it finally bottomed out into a long hollow before the bridge. Linda's Townline Diner sat on the right above the river while a long drive on the left led to his farm.

He tried to imagine how it looked to someone who had never been there before but wasn't sure he could. His family had owned this land for a couple hundred years. Hayfields covered with snow rolled away from the driveway in both directions. Maple groves for sapping broke the line of the horizon ahead. They topped that rise, and below them hundreds of acres stretched to the Somerset River. The collection of buildings—house, barns, silos, sheds—were all in good condition. He slowed the truck as they neared, pulling it close to where the gravel yard met the snow-covered lawn so Lisa wouldn't have far to walk to the door.

"Let me come around."

He climbed out and went to her side, but when she

opened the door and turned in her seat to get down, he slid his hands around her waist and helped her from the truck. Because it was high up from the ground. And because, having held her in his arms at the rink earlier, he was eager to do it again.

"Do you want the wheelchair?"

"No, I think I could use some exercise. But if you'll get my bag?"

Reluctantly, he let her go, retrieved the bag from behind the seat, and handed it to her just as a familiar scraping sound came from the side of the house. "Better watch out," he cautioned, closing the truck door and pulling her close to his side. "We've been spotted."

A painful thud preceded his favorite mongrel careening around the corner of the building and leaping up onto the front porch. Her brown hair, half ribbons of silk, half corkscrew curls, flew out from her body in every direction as she raced along the length of the porch and sailed through the air, barely coming to a stop at his feet.

"This is Sadie."

Spine bristling with excitement, she wagged her tail so fast it was a wonder she didn't get whiplash.

He bent and scooped her up into his arms before she hurt herself. "Sadie's my welcoming committee."

"I can see that." Lisa removed a mitten and reached out to stroke Sadie's back. When the dog nuzzled her palm with her wet nose, she chuckled. "What happened to her eye?"

"Raccoon." Roger squeezed Sadie close, then put her down on the ground where she danced around between them, trying to keep them in view with her one brown eye while the opaque purple one saw nothing.

"When she was a puppy, she met up with a mama raccoon under the sap house. It didn't go so well for her, and a scratch left her blind in that eye."

Lisa slid her fingers over Sadie's soft coat and rubbed her silky pointed ears. Roger admired those pretty ovals and her gentle touch.

"I love dogs."

"But you don't have one?"

"Just Mischief." Straightening, she chuckled when Sadie rolled over on the ground and lay on her back with her belly exposed.

He used the toe of his boot to scratch her underside while Sadie's front paw bounced enthusiastically with each stroke.

"I've never thought it would be fair to have a dog. I work all day. And I can't really take it out for a run, you know? I could get one that doesn't require much exercise, but…" She shrugged and trailed off. "I've got Mischief."

"I've seen that cat. I think he's the one who owns you, not the other way around."

"Truth."

Roger retrieved his foot, and Sadie rolled upright, shaking dirt off her back, then prancing in front of him on the well-worn path to the ell between the house and oldest barn. "This used to be the milk shed," he explained while holding the door open for her to enter. "Now it's mudroom, catch all, laundry." He waved to the washer and dryer in the corner.

"Why the ramps?"

"This one's always been here." He motioned to the wooden ramp with vertical stops leading to the barn. "For pushing a wheelbarrow up and down with milk.

We installed the concrete one to the house when my grandfather's arthritis took a toll and he had trouble getting up and down steps. He milked by hand."

"And that gave him arthritis?"

For answer, he dropped down into a low squat and mimicked the moves used in milking a cow. "Imagine doing this to a herd of ladies twice a day."

"Yikes."

"Right." Springing to his feet, he motioned for her to use the house ramp. "Now it's a whole different story. We still work hard, but if we're lucky, we might keep our hips and knees."

They went through the eat-in kitchen and out the back door into the enclosed porch. It was a three-season room, glass panes mounted on the inside for winter and a stack of large screens stored in the corner until spring came around again. Slatted wooden benches lined the wall closest to the house, a row of pegs above them. The large hot tub beneath a black cover dominated the center of the room.

"It looks big enough for a party."

"Trust me, the boys have had more than one out here." Going around the side, he unhooked the bar that served as a child safety lock, then flipped half the cover back to reveal steaming blue-green water. "If you want to change, the bathroom's down the hall on the left."

"Thanks."

He finished taking off the cover before going inside to his bedroom at the end of the hall. Having only toweled dry after the game, he was grungy, and a sniff of his shirt collar confirmed his need for a shower. He grabbed his swim trunks from a drawer, swapped his boots for moccasins, and waited in the hall for Lisa to emerge from the bathroom.

"Wow." He didn't even try to hide his reaction when she came out wearing a one-piece swimsuit. Swirls of sea green and burnt orange covered the white background, and a checkered band in matching colors wrapped around her rib cage just below the deep plunge of the bra top.

Putting a hand on one hip, she smirked at him. "Why, Mr. Plankey, you've got a way with words."

He couldn't help but laugh at that. Instead of being embarrassed or self-conscious, or even smug about his admiration, she threw that at him. "And you are hard on my ego."

"Something tells me you'll survive."

He reached into the closet opposite from where she stood and handed her a fluffy bath towel. "Why don't you go ahead and get started? I've got to shower the game grime off before I get in."

"Yes, sir." She moved past him, the hall wide enough for the two of them but only if she brushed against him. He pulled his stomach in to give her space, inhaling her floral scent at the same time, not surprised when his pulse kicked up a notch.

He admired her slender spine and pear-shaped bottom.

"Turn around."

"Excuse me?" Her command surprised him.

"If you get to check me out when I'm half dressed, it's only fair that I get to view your backside."

Grinning unrepentantly, he leaned down and kissed the corner of her lips. "Can't blame a guy for looking when the package is this tempting."

He might have moved in for a deeper kiss, but

Sadie pattered down the hall and wedged her way between them, rubbing against Lisa's legs and licking her fingers.

"She likes you."

"I probably smell like cat."

"C'mon, get in the hot tub before you catch cold standing around in that skimpy outfit."

"Skimpy?" She looked down at herself. "If this is skimpy, I don't know what you call some of the things I've seen at the beach."

"Indecent."

He tossed a towel onto the bathroom vanity, gripped his T-shirt behind the neck, and pulled it over his head. Only when he was sliding it off his forearms did he realize she was staring at him.

"Tell me you're not a prude."

He tossed his T-shirt onto the bench beside the tub and laughed at the idea. "I'm not a prude." He flipped his belt back to release the buckle prong before sliding the leather strip free of the loops on his jeans. "But, c'mon, you can't enjoy lying back on your towel, listening to the sound of the water, watching kids make sandcastles, and then some skinny twenty-something walks by with her ass cheeks in your face. Some tiny thong between them. Is that even sanitary?"

"They're probably clean. Just indecent, as you say."

"Hmm." He flicked the button on the top of his jeans and took the zipper tab between his thumb and finger. "I'm about to get indecent myself, so unless you want a show?"

Her cheeks went bright pink, and she hurried down the hall with Sadie.

****

Lisa stopped wondering about his opinion of swimsuits when he joined her on the porch, because she had something better to think about. Muscular thighs and calves flexing as he kicked off his moccasins. A rippling flat stomach. Long, sinewy arms bunching and releasing when he grabbed the step railings and joined her in the hot tub.

With the exception of his padded gear at the rink, she had only seen him in jeans and shirts before. Typical farmer clothing. Now that she had seen him in sport trunks, she would never be able to get the picture out of her head.

"Ooh-la-la," she said to let him know she appreciated the view.

"Oh yeah?" There was that grin again, eyes twinkling as he flexed his abs and waded closer. "Not too prudish after all?"

The navy-blue material clung to his tight buttocks and hugged his thighs. Dark swirls of hair rose from his waistband, bisecting his ribs before fanning out across his chest, and her fingers itched to touch him. Would it be soft or coarse? Was the hair dusting his thighs the same texture?

"Is that hello for me?" she couldn't help asking when her gaze fell to the front of his swimsuit, tenting now where before there had only been a bulge.

"I salute you." He didn't seem the least bit embarrassed as he slid onto the bench beside her. "What's a fella to do with such a pretty lady by his side?"

For once she didn't object to the term lady. Instead, she leaned back against the wall of the hot tub, enjoying the warmth of the water and the compliment of his reaction.

"Hmm," he murmured. "Nothing like this after a workout."

"I'll say, and all I did was watch." She stretched her legs out in front of her, enjoying the way the eddies tickled her soles.

"What happened to your toe?"

His question brought her attention to her feet, mere inches from his own, and the missing fourth toe on her right foot. As trophies for adolescent behavior went, hers was a doozy. "Bone infection."

"Ouch."

"Yeah. Remember I said I was a rebel in my teens?"

"Isn't everyone?"

"Not everyone has spina bifida, though."

"Tell me about it."

"I wanted to prove that I was 'normal.' " She made air quotes around the word with her fingers. "You know, that I could hang out with my friends and play in the snow or dance in the rain or whatever. You name it."

"But you're not like everyone else."

"No." She sighed, letting her head fall back against the tub's rim while the warm water swirled around her. "And I got my comeuppance."

"Sounds like something my grandmother would say."

She had done a little research on farming this week. To a man who dealt with udders and hock lesions, mastitis and birthing, a missing digit was probably no big deal. "Well, I got wet, my shoes rubbed against my toes, and I didn't feel a blister coming on. When I did see it, I tried to take care of it myself so my parents wouldn't find out what I'd been up to."

"And what had you been up to?"

"Skinny-dipping in the river."

"Lisa!" Hand over his heart, mock horror on his face. "I'm shocked!"

"Sure, you are." She could imagine him joining right in with the rest of them. "Anyway, by the time I told my mom about it, it was too late. The doctors tried antibiotics and creams and flushing, but the infection had gone too deep. The toe had to be amputated."

"How old were you?"

From laughter to the verge of tears in sixty seconds. That must be some kind of record, but how else was she supposed to react when he used that soft tone of voice? The one that told her he didn't buy her flippant storytelling. The one that said he knew how much losing that toe must have bothered her. And it had. It forced her to finally realize she could never be as spontaneous as she wanted to be, and her parents' worry wasn't over nothing.

"I was fifteen." She cleared the sadness from her throat. "They took it the day after my birthday."

"Ouch."

"Yeah. Ouch."

"And the allergy bracelet on your wrist? Anything I should know about?"

The thick steel band with the red star of life was not exactly her style, but necessary for survival. "Latex allergy."

"Ah." He slid over to sit at an angle to her, leaned halfway across her lap, and bent his head. "Bald spot."

A laugh bubbled out of her. Because he did actually have a coin-sized circle at the back of his head without hair, despite the rest of it being thick. She wanted very much to rub that patch of skin, but instead she asked, "Manmade or nature?"

He returned to an upright position. "Nature."

"Good to know. I was afraid you might be perfect."

"Not even close." He fingered the bracelet on her wrist. "If we ever end up in the hospital together, make sure they don't give me penicillin."

"You're allergic to it?"

"Oh yeah. So much we even have to eat organic turkey on Thanksgiving. Lots of antibiotics in their feed, you know."

She did know that. She also knew most people with his allergy could eat poultry without it being a problem. "What's your reaction?"

"To turkey? Hives, rash, itchy eyes. Doesn't kill me, but it's not much fun."

"But you don't wear a wristband or a tag?" She motioned to his neck, bare of any chain.

"Jewelry isn't a good idea for farmers. Too easy to catch it on equipment. And that *could* be deadly."

Now it was her turn to say, "Ah."

They fell into a comfortable silence then, interrupted several minutes later when the door from the kitchen swung open. Bryce ducked beneath the lintel and stepped out onto the porch. "Thought I'd find you here. Hi, Ms. Kirkpatrick."

"Hello, again."

"Good game, Pop?"

"Two zero."

"Nice. Hey, I finished raking the sand, and I was

wondering if you need me or if I can head into town for a few minutes."

"The Common Store?"

A stripe of pink colored the young man's cheeks. "How'd you guess?"

"Easy." Roger shrugged, but he didn't prolong the moment. "Yeah, go ahead, but before you leave, can you open a bottle of red and leave it on the counter for me?"

"Sure thing." He nodded to both of them. "Bye, Ms. Kirkpatrick."

When the door shut, Roger leaned his head back against the hot tub and sighed, his arm once more stretched along the rim behind her. Lisa perched a little awkwardly on the edge of her seat when his eyes closed, wondering if she should lean into him or give him space. He settled that question by cupping her shoulder and pulling her into his side.

"I could fall asleep here," he murmured.

"That's what happens when you get up at five, I guess."

"Four."

"Hmm?"

"I get up at four."

"I thought you said you have your first cup of coffee at five in the morning?"

"True. I get up at four, start the milking, and my mother gets up just before five to make a pot of coffee. She brings a mug out to me."

"Oh. So you were up last night with a cow in labor, then up again at four this morning?"

"Yep."

"How much sleep did you get?"

"About two and a half hours."

"And then you played hockey. Not an easy game, I imagine, especially if you're tired." Although he certainly seemed fit. Rugged, stocky, without much spare flesh, his body was almost as attractive as his face with the smile lines bracketing his lips and subtle streaks of silver mixed with the dark hair at his temples.

"I'm never tired on the ice. Only after. You know, when these old bones and muscles start to ache, they remind me I'm not twenty-five anymore."

"How long has it been since you were?"

One blue eye blinked open. "Fishing?"

She didn't even pretend. "Guilty."

"I'm surprised you don't remember from my registration; I'm forty-five this year."

"Definitely ancient."

Retaliating, he pulled her tight and kissed her. A long, languid kiss as warm as the steam around them. The rasp of his day beard against her neck made her quiver, and she was tempted to angle her head and give him better access, but then he sighed and leaned against the rim of the hot tub once more.

"I'm good at massage," she spontaneously offered.

"Oh?" Both eyes opened this time.

"Would you like me to rub anything down for you?"

"Now, darling, that's a loaded question if I ever heard one."

Darling. Such a simple word, used by people every day, but no one had ever used the endearment with her.

"I'm not complaining, though." He sat forward and turned slightly away from her. "I've got a kink in my back right shoulder."

Chapter Eight

"Your fingers are magic."

They were seated in the kitchen, chairs pulled up close to the wood stove and towels draped around their necks.

"Seriously." He rolled his shoulder and marveled at the loose muscles. "If you ever decide to pursue a new career, I'd recommend you."

"Glad I could help."

Leaning back, he snagged two wine glasses from the under-counter rack behind him and grabbed the open bottle of red. "Do you like wine?"

"Sure."

An indifferent reply, making him confirm before he poured, "That's a yes?"

She shrugged. "I have it on occasion."

"So you can take it or leave it?" Still uncertain, he poured a few ounces of the aromatic red into a glass and handed it to her, then served himself.

"It's not that. I just live on a budget, and alcohol is an extravagance I can't afford."

"Hmm." That made sense.

"What about you?"

"What about me?" He put the bottle on the table and sat back in his chair, cupping the glass in his hands. "Do I like wine, or do I live on a budget?"

"How about both?"

"I have a glass most nights when I finally sit down in front of the television or with a book to read."

"What do you watch?"

"Mostly documentaries. Animals. History, especially ancient history."

"Yawn." She patted her lips with her fingers as if searching for oxygen.

"And I read biographies."

"Double yawn."

"That does it." He put his glass down and pulled her chair across the floor between them until his hands rested on the wooden arms and she was trapped between his thighs. She giggled, and he leaned in to kiss her. Tasted the wine on her lips and returned for more. Sipped at the corner of her mouth, nuzzled her cheek with his nose, then blew softly on her ear. When she shivered and the skin of her upper arms pebbled, he pulled back a few inches. "Am I putting you to sleep now?"

Pushing his chest until he relaxed back into his chair again, she said, "I suddenly feel refreshed," took a drink of her wine, and rubbed the insoles of her feet along his calves.

"Temptress."

Her hazel eyes sparkled. "Tell me about the vino. You have a glass most nights?"

"Reds." He pulled the ends of her towel, drawing her close until their lips met for another long kiss before releasing her and picking up his glass again. "I don't like whites."

"And the budget?"

"Of course. I don't know anyone who has unlimited funds. We do okay here on the farm, but there are good years and bad years, like any agricultural enterprise."

"Is this year good or bad?"

"Better than last." Even the memory of that uncertain time made him grateful he was part of a family enterprise. "Farmers all over Vermont were devastated with the last economic downturn. Prices dropped, and a lot of people had to cull their herds. More than two dozen farms folded up in one year alone."

"How did you get through it?"

"We're not out of the woods yet, but we're frugal." A lesson learned over generations. "We spend money on the business—you know, regular upkeep, improvements, preventive maintenance. Money is only spent on personal stuff after the farm is taken care of. We're also risk averse, as far as debt goes, and always diversifying our operations to protect against loss."

Lisa took a sip of wine and rolled the glass in her hand. The vintage colored her lips a dark red, and he wanted to swoop in and lick them clean again, but he was already testing the dimensions of his swimwear.

"So do you even make as much as your hired help?"

"Who's the smart lady?" He chuckled, surprised by her insight, because some years it was close. "We can't run a farm this size without employees."

"You must save on expenses, though, all living together."

"Hmm. What about you? Was money a concern in your household?"

"A concern?" she repeated. "No. Hard to be concerned about something you never see. It also didn't mean anything to my parents, so they never worried about it. That's not the same thing as having some."

"So you're careful with your spending?"

"I bought my house on a short sale. And you've seen my car, eight years old this spring, and I plan to get at least ten out of it. I spend money like I don't have any."

"That's why you work the second job?"

"Second. Third." He raised his eyebrows in inquiry, and she reminded him, "My jewelry business. Everything from the town goes into my savings. It's not a lot, because I usually only work one Saturday a month, but it's something. I use the jewelry money for personal stuff. Manicures." She waved the dark red ovals and flint corn tips at him. "Though Jonnie does them now, so I only pay for supplies. I use the rest of the revenue for clothes, makeup. Sometimes flowers for the table."

"So you're a flower girl."

"A wet one at the moment." She plucked at the fabric of her swimsuit where it bunched around her waist. "I need to get out of this."

"Do you need any help?"

"In broad daylight?" She looked scandalized.

"And you called me a prude."

They shared a smile, but he relented, waving toward the bathroom. "Knock yourself out. There should be a blow-dryer beneath the vanity if you want to use it."

She moved in that direction, and he watched her go. Despite their earlier flirtation in the hallway, he could tell she was a little self-conscious about her body, but to his way of thinking, there was nothing wrong with it. Her torso was lean, her breasts small but ample. Her bottom half was wider than the top, but women were often built that way, and she was all woman. Her toned thighs and slender calves made him want to drop to his knees and run his fingers up the length of them.

"You wouldn't be checking out my backside again, would you?" she threw over her shoulder.

"And what if I am?"

For answer, she scuttled backward until she was in the doorway between the kitchen and hall, put both hands on her hips, and said, "Then I'll walk slower this time."

****

He was still smiling over that when they returned to the kitchen dressed in their regular clothes. Picking up both wineglasses, he motioned to the room on the other side of the front entry hall. "Would you like to finish in the parlor?"

"Parlor? Is that really a word nowadays?" she asked even as she followed him past the staircase into the other room.

"We used to have both a parlor and a living room. The name stuck."

He offered her one of two easy chairs beside a coffee table, but she seemed more interested in the family photos covering much of the wall space. He wasn't surprised when she went to inspect one in particular.

"Is this you and Mindy?"

"Yes. On our wedding day."

"Had she already changed out of her dress when this was taken?"

"No." Although the photo was now twenty-plus

years old, he remembered that day like yesterday. The smell of rectangular hay bales set up as seats for their guests. The echo of the live band in the field. The sizzle of pig roasting on a spit over the bonfire. The bitter taste of beer from the keg.

"Mindy was a farm girl. Her whole family is involved in it. Her sister works for UVM Extension, and her brother is an inspector for the Agency of Agriculture. I still see him for work and hockey. He was at the rink this morning. Big blond guy named Chase."

She nodded at his description.

"Anyway, we wanted the wedding to represent who we are and where we come from, but the outfits were her idea."

They both looked at the couple in the picture. Him with a pitchfork in hand and a dopey grin on his face, her with a giant brooch at her neck and the devil in her eye, the two of them barely able to hold their poses. "Do you know the painting?"

"American Gothic? Yes. I'm not sure you carried off the somber tone of it, though."

"We were rarely serious." Just two kids, happy and hopeful. Unaware of what life had in store for them a few years down the road.

The sound of the mudroom door opening had them turning in that direction. Footsteps crossed the floor, and his mother came into the parlor.

"Hi, Maman. How are the new calves?"

"Good." She pulled a pin from her silver-streaked bun, and it fell in a long swath midway down her back. "Hello, Lisa."

"Hi, Mrs. Plankey."

"I'm going to take a shower. Darcy's in the calf barn with Zeb, but we've got another cow in labor. Your father and Tony are with her now."

"That means I'm needed."

"Oh! Of course."

They drained their glasses and put them in the kitchen sink on their way out. Sadie joined them in the truck after sitting beside it, whining while he helped Lisa up into the passenger seat.

"Someone is well trained," she noted.

"Yeah. I'm a sucker for a pretty gal."

****

"Jonnie, it was so much fun!" Lisa kept her hands in the bowl of sudsy water on her dining table when she really wanted to get up and dance around the room. Even talking about her date yesterday had her so amped up she could barely sit still.

"We only have an hour. Better give me all the details."

Lisa recounted their time at the rink. How strong he was, holding her close and gliding across the ice with so little effort, as if her extra weight was nothing. And the way he lifted her and flipped her around. She still couldn't believe how easily he'd done that.

"He must be really strong if he can pick *you* up," Jonnie teased, and they both laughed.

"Okay, so I don't weigh two hundred pounds or anything, but still."

"How much does a cow weigh?" Jonnie asked while removing one hand from the water and applying an orangewood stick to the cuticles.

"What? I have no idea."

"Hmm, you're probably nothing compared to what

he's used to."

"Would you be serious here? The man has some muscles. I never knew I was into that sort of thing, but it was like flying. Like…" She stopped, lost for words.

"Like being free."

At Jonnie's comment, she collapsed against her chair back. "Exactly."

Neither one of them said anything for a long time. That was a powerful word to a person whose movements had been monitored and curtailed by others. She knew Jonnie understood as no one else could, though their circumstances were different. Jonnie was physical, hyperactive even, but she'd spent her childhood trying to *be good*, which meant not running around, jumping up and down, or touching things even though she craved every one of those tactile experiences. Lisa was always good, her short-lived attempt at rebellion notwithstanding, yet she'd grown up in someone else's image of what she should be.

"So what's the problem?" Jonnie finally asked.

"I'm scared."

"Because it's perfect?"

Only Jonnie would understand enough to ask that question. She had found her *Mr. Right*, and she would know just how terrifying it could be. Was Lisa imagining this thing between herself and Roger? He had kissed her a few times. She got warm all over when he was close. Talking to him was easy. Everything was easy.

"I'm afraid it might be too perfect."

"Well, look at me. I found my ideal man and almost let him get away. Then someone asked me if I'd lost my mind."

Lisa cringed, remembering her question when Jonnie had first accepted David's proposal of marriage. "I'm surprised you're still talking to me after that."

"You wouldn't be a true friend if you hadn't asked the question. So have you lost your mind?"

"No."

"And do you know what the hell you're doing?"

"Not a clue."

****

She was feeling a little more confident when he came over for dinner on Wednesday evening. A late meal, since he had to finish the milking and wash up before driving to her house, which gave her time to drop off a dish at the church potluck supper, even though she couldn't stay for the Bible study that followed. Lucky for her, Hazel was busy talking with someone and couldn't give her grief for that.

"No Sadie this time," Roger assured her when she opened the door to him. Their goodbye in the truck the other day had lingered so long the dog finally nudged herself between them and licked Lisa's face. A surefire way to kill an amorous mood.

They had spoken every night since, but this was the first time she'd seen him in person, and if his kiss of greeting was any indication, he had missed that contact as much as she had.

"Smells good," he said when they came up for air.

"Hope you like lasagna?"

He removed his hat and shucked his coat. "I do, but I wasn't talking about the food."

She took his things and laid them over the back of the sofa, then wrapped her arms around his middle. Buried her nose in the shoulder of his plaid button-down shirt and inhaled deeply. "Hmm, you're not so bad yourself."

He dipped his head for another kiss, but Mischief came slinking around the side of the kitchen island and yowled plaintively before padding over to butt his head against the back of her knee. "I sense a pet theme to our relationship."

****

"You were saying something about pets?" she asked when he stopped by her craft table at Somerset Academy Saturday morning after attending the Veterans' Day breakfast in the cafeteria.

He held up a pair of paw-print cufflinks from her table. "Do these things sell?"

"Like hot cakes. These are even more popular." She pointed to several earrings with similar designs. "And I just started making these, but already today I have six orders." She held out an open-wrap silver bracelet with a heart on one end and a paw on the other. "I inscribe the dog's name for them and the date if they've crossed the rainbow bridge."

"Nice." He returned the cuff links to their velvet display back and winked. "But the prettiest thing here is sitting behind the table."

Her face warmed at the compliment. When he leaned over the expanse of jewelry to kiss her cheek, that heat spread down to the rest of her body.

"Still on for tonight's card party?"

She waved her nails at him, red, white, and blue stripes across the tips except for the index fingers, each bearing a silver star. "I'll be there with flags on."

They took separate cars. This time she found open parking on the same side of the road as the building, so he saw her from the ramp when she pulled in and hurried to help with her wheelchair. Most of the snow had melted since the storm the other night, but it made a slushy mess in daytime that froze into crusty, uneven ridges at sundown. Hard to navigate in a wheelchair. He pushed her around the hurdles while she kept two pans of food safe in her lap.

"Make anything good?" he asked.

"Apple cider biscuits and apple walnut slaw."

"Those were delicious," Darcy told her when the meal ended. She had once again joined them after selling admission and 50/50 tickets. "Can you teach me to cook?"

"Whoa, pumpkin," Roger objected, but Lisa put a hand on his arm and stopped him.

"I'd love to, but wouldn't it be easier to ask your grandmother?"

The teen exchanged a glance with her uncle. "Mémère doesn't like to cook."

"No?" Surprised, Lisa looked from one to the other. "Isn't that some sort of prerequisite for being a farmer's wife? You know, cooking and canning and everything."

Roger shrugged. "She does it; she just doesn't enjoy it. Especially the baking. Says it's one more chore and she'd rather be in the barn or in the garden. So the canning is a yes, the cooking not so much."

"And your aunt, Linda?"

"She's a great cook, but when she's done at the diner, she doesn't want to see the inside of a kitchen. Her words." Darcy scooped the 50/50 ticket money from the belt around her waist and started counting it. "It's okay if you don't want to."

"I'd love to," Lisa repeated, flattered the teen would ask her. "When can you come over?"

While Roger left to help take down the long tables and put up the smaller ones used for the card party, she and Darcy arranged to meet at her house on Tuesday after she got home from work and volleyball practice was over.

"Are you sure about this?" he asked when his niece hurried across the room to put the tickets in the tumbler for drawing. "Don't feel obligated to say yes."

"Heck no. I like that girl."

"Well, I like her, too, but you said yourself you're busy with craft shows at this time of year, and I don't want you biting off more than you can chew."

"Come here." She crooked her index finger for him to bend low as if to whisper something to him. When his cheek touched hers, she turned her head and nipped his ear.

He jerked upright and frowned at her.

"I only bite when the mood strikes me."

His slow smile made her insides clench and her imagination soar even before he said, "Lisa, Lisa, what am I going to do with you?"

"I can think of a few things."

"Number 8-0-1-5-9-A," Dougie announced. "The winner is 8-0-1-5-9-A."

"That's me!"

She rarely won anything. Except for the kitty whist booby prize, which she took home for the second time. When Dougie realized she had already been given a pair of slinky glasses, he suggested she pick something else from their little store of prizes.

"Not a chance." She clutched the plastic spectacles

to her chest. "I need these for my collection."

Chapter Nine

"Sure smells good in here," Roger said on stepping into her house Tuesday evening, "and this time I do mean the food."

He could get used to this, coming home to her after his evening chores.

"Uncle Roger, wait until you taste this!" Darcy stepped forward with something in her hand, but he held a finger up to make her pause, bypassing her to kiss Lisa first.

When he turned back to his niece, her eyes and mouth were round, and a blush stained her cheeks. "Sorry, I didn't mean to…"

She didn't seem to know how to finish the sentence, compounding her embarrassment.

"No problem. You've got something for me to try?"

"The best apple turnovers on the planet. I made some with extra cinnamon, since Abby loves anything with cinnamon, and she cooks okay, but she's not much of a baker, either, not like Lisa here. Oh! And next week we're going to make crepes, because I told Lisa how much Abby loves fresh fruit, and you can put just about anything in crepes—"

"Can I get a bite today, pumpkin?"

"Here." She all but shoved a turnover into his hand before retreating to the kitchen. "We'll do the dishes,

Lisa."

"You don't have to."

"Yes, we do," Chelsea insisted on emerging from the bathroom. He hadn't known she was learning to cook, too.

"Hi, Mr. Plankey. I mean Roger."

"Besides, we used your ingredients, so I owe you." Darcy put the drain stopper in the sink and turned on the faucet. "Pop said to make sure I bring what we need next time so you're not out any money."

Chelsea scraped flour from the kitchen island into her palm and dropped it in the trash can. "I'll buy food for the week after that."

"So this is going to be a regular thing?" Roger asked Lisa.

She shrugged. "At least until we run out of recipes to try."

The doorbell rang, and everyone turned to look at the portal.

"Who would be here at this hour?" Lisa wondered.

"I'll get it." Darcy left the sink filling with water and opened the door, only to retreat almost instantly back to the kitchen without saying a word.

Paul Weatherbee stepped over the threshold. "Hey, Ms. Kirkpatrick. Sorry it's so late, but I've got your Christmas wreaths. You want me to put them in the same place as last year?"

"That would be perfect, but can you do it with one arm?"

He held his cast up, a cocksure grin on his face. "You'd be surprised what I can accomplish with only one."

"Okay, but only if you help Roger with our taste

testing. Do you like cinnamon?"

"Love it."

"Darcy, why don't you give him one of those you made with extra cinnamon?"

His niece went pale, then pink, her hands frozen in the sudsy water while the young man waited for his sample. Chelsea finally nudged her into action.

Not saying a word, unusual in itself, Darcy dried her hands on a dish towel, then scooped one of the tarts off the waxed paper they cooled on. She almost dropped it trying to avoid any physical contact with Paul Weatherbee. Only his quick reflexes, one-handed at that, kept it from hitting the floor.

Roger stuffed his face with pastry to avoid laughing at the obvious tension between the two while Lisa scolded him with a look.

****

"Any new calves this week?" she remembered to ask when he dropped her off after the weekly supper and kitty-whist party. Empty-handed this time since her game had improved enough to avoid winning the booby prize.

"Five."

"Wow, you have been busy. Lucky for me you could get away for the night."

"Hmm." He leaned across the center console and ran a finger down her cheek. "I'd rather be busy with you."

She turned her face into his kiss, wishing for once they didn't have to go their separate ways. "What about luck?"

"What do you mean?"

"I mean, do you want to get lucky? With me?"

"Darling, every day of the week and twice on Sunday."

Despite that affirmation, a few minutes later he flashed his headlights in goodbye, and she waved to him from the window, already looking forward to seeing him tomorrow. He was picking her up after the hockey game for a tour of the calving barn.

But instead of Roger stopping at her house just after lunch, Hazel showed up.

"This is a surprise." They had seen one another at church and chatted a little bit afterward, so she wondered what brought her sister here now.

"I know." Stepping into the house, Hazel bent and gave Mischief a quick rub when he came to see who was disturbing his Sunday nap. He arched his back and swatted her palm, then retreated to the hobby room. Leaving her standing awkwardly on the welcome mat.

"Better spit it out."

"What makes you think I have something on my mind?"

Lisa barely refrained from rolling her eyes like Darcy. "You haven't taken your coat off. We saw each other an hour ago. Obviously, something has come up between then and now."

Hazel sighed. "I'm sorry, but I've been asked to do a funeral for the Evans family. I won't be able to take you to your appointment in Syracuse."

"Oh."

Like so many people with spina bifida, the moment she turned eighteen, the pediatric clinic had cut her loose. Suddenly she'd found herself having to assemble her own team of doctors to monitor her health, only none of them were in the same practice, and trying to coordinate communication between them had been a nightmare.

"Well. That sucks." What else could she say? She had spent years searching for an adult spina bifida clinic, finally locating this one at Upstate University Hospital. She went once annually and saw local doctors in between visits.

"Maybe you could reschedule?"

Another nightmare. The hospital was an eight-hour drive from Somerset. Getting a different appointment was not as much a problem as arranging her work schedule to have two full days off during the week because the long trip required an overnight stay.

"I'll see if Roger can help me." She was thinking aloud, not really talking to her sister, but it was either him or Jonnie, and her best friend had four little boys to care for. Yet he had the farm. Work that required his attention seven days a week. He had his family and the hired help, but could they cover him for two days? Would he even want to make the trip with her?

"You have been spending a lot of time together."

Hazel's statement brought her rumination to an end. Was that a judgment disguised as an observation?

"What about it?" Lisa tried to remain calm. Really, she did.

"I mean, do you think that's a good idea?"

"What's that supposed to mean?" Hackles raised. All pretense of calm gone.

"I mean, you've been seeing a lot of this guy. That's great, I'm glad you like his company and everything, but this is kind of personal business, don't you think?"

Lisa was a happy person. She liked people, laughed

a lot, and generally enjoyed life. But her sister could fire her temper quicker than a lit match in a barn full of dry hay. "Because kissing him isn't personal or anything," she snapped. "Not to mention some of the rubbing and grinding we do."

"Don't be crude."

"Then don't be a prude."

Hazel shook her head, like their mother did when she was exasperated. "Well, one of us has to be practical about this. Do you really think it's a good idea to start something with him?"

"Explain yourself."

"Does he know you might not have a full life expectancy?"

"Low blow, little sister."

"I'm not trying to be mean. Really, I'm not, but have you had those conversations? You know, the serious ones, not just the roses-and-sunshine stuff."

"It hasn't come up over coffee yet."

"Then it should." Hazel ran her fingers through her brown hair. It was usually a neat bob with not a single strand out of place. She only played with it when she was really stressed, so this conversation was upsetting her as much as it was Lisa, but for once Lisa didn't care.

"It's my life. My romance. I'll manage it the way I see fit."

"Now you're being stubborn. Instead of thinking about yourself, try thinking about him. Are you being fair to him?"

Someone honked a horn in the driveway.

Hazel pulled the living room curtain aside, said, "Speaking of your farmer friend," and let the curtain fall back into place. "Well, good luck with your appointment. Let me know if you reschedule and need a ride."

She opened the door, barely acknowledging Roger with a glance on her way out.

"Have you been here long?" Lisa's voice came out an octave higher than usual.

"Long enough to wonder if I should get you two boxing gloves."

"Sorry about that." Her shoulders sagged on a heavy exhale. Even a short argument with her sister was exhausting.

"I could hear you over the diesel engine. Didn't seem like knocking was a good idea."

At least he hadn't turned and run. "I'll get my coat."

"Do you want to talk about it?" he asked on the way to the farm.

"Nope."

"Okay, then."

He didn't say anything else until they were parked in his front yard. There he came around, pulled the passenger door open wide, and slid his hands around her waist, helping her out of the truck and down onto her feet. She held on to the door handle until she found her balance.

"Do you want the wheelchair or your crutches?"

Most of the snow from the early storm had melted, and the ground was hard with only a dusting of white over brown and gold leaves. "Crutches should be okay."

"All right, but let me know if you change your mind." He pulled the aluminum forearm crutches out from behind the bench seat, and she slid them on. When she would have taken a step away from the truck so he could close the door, he bent low until his face was at the same level as hers, his blue eyes serious when he said, "I mean it, Lisa. If you get all tired out, you'll pay for it, and I'll catch hell from that sister of yours."

"You've only met her once. You don't even know her yet."

"But I will. In the meantime, don't be foolish. I already know you're brave and independent. You don't have to prove anything to me."

If it wasn't such a nice compliment, she might have objected to his well-meant condescension. Instead, she gave him a salute, said, "Aye, aye, sir," and when he moved out of the way, "Please carry on with the tour."

Grinning at her imperial manner, he bowed and flourished a hand in the direction of the milk shed, but before she could start on that path, Sadie came barreling around the corner of the house, raced across the porch, and leaped off the end.

"Sadie, girl." When she skidded to a stop in front of him, he ran a hand over her silky head and down her back. "Don't forget to say hello to Lisa."

The dog turned and sat on her haunches with her face lifted. Waiting patiently for adoration.

"Hello, beautiful." She fingered Sadie's silky ears and scratched beneath her chin. The dog's brown eye closed with pleasure while the purple one remained partially open.

"I thought we'd start with the main barn first."

Sadie pulled away and padded ahead of them toward the milk shed entrance.

"Though it might not be what you expect."

That was obvious from the moment she stepped into the building. For one thing, it was enormous. For another, the image in her mind was of lofts spilling loose hay above wooden box stalls holding a couple dozen cows. Maybe like what she'd seen at fairgrounds. Instead, at least a hundred cows filled the open space, their black-and-white faces poking out between aluminum partitions, eating hay from a narrow lane in front of them.

By the time they made it to the end of the building, she had an entirely new vocabulary. They were in the alley. The cows were in a free stall. The sides of the barn were curtains that could be raised and lowered to accommodate temperature changes. Cows weighed between a thousand pounds and one ton each. If her eyes could have popped out of her head, as the expression went, they would have.

"No wonder you picked me up like I weighed nothing at the ice rink."

"You're just a little thing compared to my girls here."

"Gee, thanks. I've always wanted to be compared to a cow."

"You're cuter." He grinned, tapping her nose with his finger. "And you smell better."

"Such a charming guy."

The back door swung open, and two men entered, the sunlight behind them making it impossible to see who they were until they closed the door. She recognized Bryce but not the other one.

"Hey, boys," Roger greeted. "Colin, I don't think you've met my friend Lisa. Lisa, this is Glen's son."

She might have guessed. Not only was he tall like

his father and cousin, but he was a looker, too. Dark-brown waves flopped over light-blue eyes, and his smile would make any girl's heart pitter-patter.

"We've met before," he said.

"We have?"

"At David and Jonnie's wedding. You were the maid of honor."

"That's right."

"I remember because you rolled up to the ceremony in a wheelchair. And I never forget a pretty face."

Roger gave him a soft punch on the shoulder. "Down, boy."

"Where were you when I was a teenager?" she teased.

"Just an apple in his father's eye, if that, which makes him jailbait." To his nephew he added, "And she's off-limits."

The door banged open behind them, and Darcy stormed in. Cheeks ruddy. Eyes flashing. "They left me in the hayloft!"

Roger wrapped his arm around the irate girl's shoulders and pulled her against his side. "You okay, pumpkin?" At her reluctant nod, he turned a stern look on the young men. "What have I told you two about treating her right?"

"It's her fault," Colin complained. "She wouldn't shut up about our girlfriends."

"Oh yeah"—Darcy turned in his embrace—"speaking of girlfriends, Betsy is looking for you."

"Okay, I'll go see her."

What? Who is Betsy?

"Don't think I didn't hear them, though. If you're

picking on them about the girls in their lives, I'll tell them about the boy in yours."

"What?" Darcy spun out of his embrace and all but stomped her foot. "Uncle Roger!"

"She has a boyfriend?"

"Who is it?"

Roger pushed the back door open and motioned for Lisa to go out before him. "Think that'll keep them busy for a while?"

"You're mean." But she enjoyed the byplay between the four of them and the irrepressible twinkle in his eyes. When he didn't say anything else, she walked with him along the bumpy path to a second barn. "Does she really have a boyfriend?"

"I don't think so, but if I had to guess, I'd say she has a thing for the Weatherbee boy."

"Paul? She doesn't even like him."

Roger grinned and opened the door to the next building. "Exactly. But even if she doesn't *like* him, it might make her think twice about teasing the boys. She has a tendency to speak first, regret later."

"But you love her."

"One of my favorite people on the planet."

She made no reply because just then a loud bleating noise assailed her ears, and she cringed in the doorway. "What on earth is that?"

"That's Betsy."

"Betsy's a cow?"

"I'll show you."

They were in the calf barn, she realized, as they passed dozens of babies with ear tags and big dark eyes before coming to a single stall with a solid wood door. "You'll want to lean against the wall."

Lisa moved back and pulled her crutches in close to her body.

"Here she comes." He unlatched the door, and a black-and-white cow stumbled out into the alley, almost falling over before righting herself on three legs.

Three legs! Lisa had never seen a handicapped bovine before. If she had given it any thought, she would have assumed a three-legged cow would be euthanized at birth. Yet here was this one, at least four times the size of those in the free stall, butting Roger in the side with her head until he relented and wrapped his arms around her neck in a big hug.

"That's my girl," he crooned, rubbing his cheek against her jaw and stroking her neck with his hand. "That's my good Bets."

The cow sighed. Did cows even sigh? Whatever the noise was, it was as close to one as any word could describe.

"How did you end up with a disabled cow?"

"Bets' mother cast her withers after her birth."

Lisa had no idea what that meant, so she raised her eyebrows and waited for further explanation.

"She had a prolapsed uterus. That means it comes out with the afterbirth. She died before she could even lick Betsy's face. Poor Bets was tangled up on the way out, and her leg got twisted. It was either put her to sleep or have it amputated."

"You paid a vet to remove her leg? Wouldn't it have been easier to let her go, too?"

"I'd been up with her and her mother all night long. A bitter-cold night, too. Just about froze my hand off from having it inside the cow trying to help this little girl out. The vet was over in Canaan on a farm call and couldn't get here, not in the middle of the snowstorm we were having. I did the best I could, but it wasn't good enough."

"And you, what? Fell in love with her as soon as she was born?"

"More like she stole my heart."

Lisa took a cautious step forward, then another, until she could tentatively stroke the heifer's head between her slanted dark eyes.

"Well, I'll be damned."

"What?"

"Bets doesn't normally share me with other people."

"She gets jealous?" Lisa asked with disbelief. "A cow?"

"Bets isn't just any cow."

The three-legged female proved that as she followed them the length of the alley, hugging his side and nudging him whenever he went too long between petting her. If the cow could dance on three legs, she probably would when he offered her a lick from the salt block by the door before they turned and went back down the alley. At some point Sadie pushed her way into the building and joined them.

Roger coaxed Betsy back into her stall but leaned over the half wall to give her some more affection. Sadie jumped up beside him, front paws on the top of the door, and licked the cow's ear.

What a tableau they must make. An able-bodied man with a three-legged cow, a long-haired, half-blind mongrel, and a woman on crutches.

"I feel like I should be in that movie about defective toys," Lisa murmured. "You know, the

Christmas special?"

He gave Betsy one last stroke and rejoined her, Sadie prancing along beside them, her brown hair floating up and down with each move. "You're not defective."

Lisa shrugged. "You know what I mean."

"I stand by my statement."

Changing the subject, because she didn't want to ruin what was an otherwise good afternoon by arguing over something when she appreciated his viewpoint more than her own anyway, she asked, "How long can a cow live with three legs? I mean, if she ends up weighing half a ton or more?"

"I don't know, but we'll find out."

"Wouldn't it be easier to turn her into hamburger?"

He stopped. Put his hands on her shoulders, leaned in, and kissed her. Pulled back a little, said, "Watch your tongue," and kissed her some more. When he finally let her go, Sadie was lying on the floor at his feet, Betsy was mooing plaintively from her stall, and Lisa forgot what they had been talking about.

Chapter Ten

"Welcome to my parlor." Roger opened the door to the next barn.

"Said the spider to the fly," Lisa paraphrased the old poem, then came to a stop when she saw the inside of the building. "Wow."

"Not what you pictured, is it?"

"You can say that again."

"Not what you—"

He didn't finish because she slugged him playfully on the arm.

"I can see why you made Sadie stay outside."

The place was spotless. A stray dog hair would definitely be noticed and, she imagined, not sanitary. The room was dominated by a circular parlor with shallow steps for the cows to get on and off. Round steel tanks along the back wall stored milk until the truck came for it.

"When is that?"

"Ten o'clock in the morning, every other day."

"How do you keep it from going bad?"

"Temperature is thirty-six degrees, in the tanks and in the truck or tanker, and the milk is stirred frequently. The driver tests it before taking it to the processing plant. When we go outside, you'll see some massive generators. We can't afford to lose power even for a day."

"The cows come in from the barn through that door?"

He nodded, showing her the connecting ramp between the two buildings, divided into two lanes, one coming in, one going out.

"You say ramps, but they're almost flat. More like chutes."

"Cows don't do well with inclines. Going up is okay, but down is an issue."

"I've got the same problem."

He took her hand and squeezed it. "Like I said, you're a lot cuter than a cow."

"You're a charmer, Mr. Farmer."

"Just come up with that one?"

"Right off the top of my head." She was fast losing her heart to this man. Part of her worried because it was too easy, while another part admonished herself for looking a gift horse in the mouth. Or gift cow, as the case might be.

"Want to see the rest?"

"Of course."

Outside the milking parlor sat two four-wheelers and a golf cart. "I figured we could ride around the property. Which one of these would you prefer?"

"Easy answer." She went directly to one of the ATVs, slipped her crutches off, and propped them against the wall beside the barn door.

"You know how to drive one of these?"

"Not a clue."

"One of the things I like about you, darling. You're always game."

****

In fact, he liked quite a few things about this

woman. Her friendliness with everyone. Her generosity of spirit, the way she entertained Preston, doted on Jonnie's kids, taught Darcy and Chelsea to bake. Her forthright nature. Her celebratory style.

Yet even as he crossed the highway to introduce her to Zeb and Carolyn and show her their part of the property, he wondered what she and her sister had argued about. It was the first time he'd seen her truly upset. He hoped she could trust him enough to share more than just good times.

"That was exactly what I needed today," she said when they returned the four-wheelers to the barn. "Thank you."

"You're welcome."

She fiddled with the key, gazing out at the silver domed silos on the other side of the main barn, then back at him. "You asked if I wanted to talk about it."

He waited, hoping to encourage her with silence.

"I have an appointment in Syracuse on Tuesday afternoon. An annual thing. My sister usually takes me, but she has a funeral and can't drive me this time."

"Long drive." Miserable one, too, in his opinion, unless he was going to the Finger Lakes for his family's annual fishing vacation.

"Yes."

"So you need a driver?"

"I do."

The question in her eyes mixed with her clear reluctance to ask it.

"Would you like me to take you there?" Miserable though it was, he would make the journey for her.

"It's a two-day trip unless you drive through the night."

126

"Bryce and Colin are both home from college for Thanksgiving. This is probably the best possible time for me to be gone a couple of days."

"You're sure?"

"I wouldn't offer otherwise. Is that what you and your sister argued about?"

She nodded. "Hazel doesn't want me taking advantage of you."

He climbed off his vehicle, straddled the back of her ATV, and pulled her into the cradle of his thighs. "Maybe I'm the one taking advantage of you." He kissed the side of her neck. "Maybe I'm just getting started."

She let out a squeak when he started the ignition and the ATV shot forward. Around the corner of the barn. Across the back lawn to the front yard. Up the long drive and across the ridge to the sugar shack.

"Wanna go four-wheeling?"

"I thought that's what we were doing."

"Not yet. Better hold on tight."

He wove in and out of the maple trees and down the steep hill into a copse of evergreens. Their land abutted the Weatherbee property, and Dottie let the boys make trails through her tree farm. Though he didn't normally take advantage of that, today he did.

The air was brisk. Even in the shelter of the woods, it bit into his cheeks and made his eyes water. He checked on Lisa often to make sure she wasn't too cold.

"I'm having the time of my life!" she shouted, leaning back to kiss him while squeezing his thighs. "Don't stop now."

They rode through a hundred acres of forest, then came to a large clearing above Weatherbee Pond. A small, dark body of water, it was warmer than Somerset Lake or the river. "This will be a campground on this side. No sites on the back, though. That's our swimming hole."

"Yours, as in your family?"

"We share ownership with Dottie Weatherbee. See the rope swing?"

Normally it dangled above the water a few yards from the dock. Today it was hooked on a tree branch, the last swimmer having left it there for the next person to use. Pieces of wood nailed to the tree trunk beneath it made a ladder of sorts up to that spot.

"How many campsites will she have?"

"Two dozen, all told."

"When does it open?"

"This summer. She's going to put an in-ground swimming pool here, where we are, and build a clubhouse with restrooms and showers, but she should be ready by the Fourth of July." He squeezed her waist and dropped his voice. "Guess that means if you want to go skinny-dipping with me, we'll have to do it before the end of June."

Her loud, throaty laughter scared a flock of bohemian waxwings from a nearby elderberry bush. That made her laugh some more, stopping only when he swooped in for a kiss. One that went from fun and sweet to hot and spicy in a matter of seconds.

"June it is," she purred. "Under a full moon. I'll mark it on my calendar."

He revved the engine—what else was a man to do—and drove through some more trees until they came out into the Weatherbee yard.

Dottie emerged from her chicken coop to greet

them. "Hey, Slick."

"Hey, Dottie." Killing the engine, he unfolded himself from the four-wheeler and helped Lisa to her feet. "Nice day."

"Hmm. Looks like the next snow's holding off until the weekend, anyway." She checked the skies the way people did when trying to predict the weather by the shape and color of the clouds.

"Do you know Lisa Kirkpatrick?"

"Not formally, but I've heard a lot about you from Paul. Nice to meet you."

"You, too. How is he doing?"

"Trying to keep up with his schoolwork one-handed. He's with his tutor right now."

At that moment the young man came out of the house, but he wasn't alone.

"Uncle Roger!"

****

"I told you there was something going on with the two of them. And not just tutoring."

"Smart man." Lisa wasn't proud, and she didn't mind admitting he was right while she had completely misread the tension between the teenagers. "Thanks again for stopping."

"No problem." They had left her house right after he finished milking on Tuesday morning and were now heading west on Autoroute 10 between Sherbrooke and Montreal.

Without asking, he had pulled into a gas station on the pretense of stretching his legs. She knew it had really been for her to use the restroom, because this was the second stop since they'd hit the road, the first one on the pretext of eating the crepes she had packed. Both times just happened to coincide with her normal lavatory schedule.

"Why don't you choose a radio station?" he suggested.

She scanned available frequencies only to realize how few choices she had. While she and Hazel took the longer route through Albany for fear of breaking down in Quebec and not being able to communicate, French Canadian was Roger's second language. The extent of her vocabulary ended at *oui*, *bonjour*, and *merci*. Not helpful when the only stations playing anything approaching rock music used a broader collection of words.

"I guess I assumed they'd be in English."

She finally gave up and switched off the radio, relaxing into the passenger seat of his mother's car. He'd borrowed it for the trip because it was roomier and more comfortable than her own and better on gas than his truck.

"Tell me about your folks."

No longer relaxed, she slid her gaze to him, but his eyes were on the road ahead. It was just an idle question, then, but as a minister's kid, she had learned not to lead with her parents' occupation. Or to introduce Hazel by hers. People in some parts of the country assumed she was a wonderful person by virtue of association, but in other parts of the country, New England in particular, they assumed something entirely different, and more than one budding friendship had been snuffed out the instant she shared that information.

So she simply said, "They live in Philadelphia. Retired, but they're still busy."

"What do they do with all their free time?"

"Volunteer at a soup kitchen and homeless shelter."

"The thrift store wasn't an exception, then."

"What thrift store?"

"You said they volunteered at one when you were younger, and that's how you started making costumes and coming up with your own fashion style."

Oh. She had told him that, hadn't she? "I'm surprised you remember."

"Like an elephant." He tapped a finger to his temple. "I never forget."

"You're much better looking than an elephant."

"Keep it up." He grinned. "Flattery will get you pretty much anything."

Easing back into the seat cushions again, she smiled and looked out the window at the passing scenery. Despite the brown season, she enjoyed traveling through the hills of the Eastern Townships and around Lake Memphremagog. She wished they could have stopped at the park on the Canadian side, because it was beautiful and looked wheelchair friendly.

"Do you stay in touch with your parents?" he asked, returning to their conversation.

"We talk once a week. Usually on Sunday nights, but we're not exactly close."

"No?"

Sighing, she turned away from the landscape. "We don't have any problems, but I'm almost forty years old. My life is up here. Their lives are in Pennsylvania. We were never as close as you are with your family, but I love them, and I know they love me. If I really needed something, they'd be here for me and vice versa."

"Hmm." He paused while overtaking an eighteen-wheeler struggling to conquer an incline. "And is it just you and Hazel? No other siblings?"

"Just the two of us." Before he could ask, she explained, "I came to Somerset first. She helped me move here and, when she saw the apartment I rented, stayed until she could find something better for me. That took a few months, and by then she decided it was a nice place to live, so..." She raised her hands to indicate he knew the rest of the story.

From there the conversation turned to his family, and he filled in some missing gaps for her. His oldest son, Trevor, had been six when Mindy died of breast cancer. Bryce had been a toddler and had no memories of her. Ironic, he said, because Bryce was so much like her in looks, temperament, and interests.

"He and Colin are the next generation of the farm. They're both in college now, but they'll run it together. When that happens, Zeb and Carolyn will retire to South Carolina to be close to their daughter and grandchildren. Mom and Dad will move into their house and take over running the calf barn, and that will leave room in the main house for the boys to start their own families."

"Nice continuity. What else do you pass down from generation to generation?"

"Douglas."

"Hmm?"

"The first son's middle name is always Douglas. Dad, me, Trevor. Glen's ex-wife wouldn't let him use it for Colin, but his baby is Justin Douglas Plankey. The boys plan to use it for their firstborn, too."

"Nice." Lisa had never given much thought to things like that, being from a small family herself and female on top of it. If she had ever married, her last name would have changed, and any children would have been something other than Kirkpatrick.

They were quiet for a few minutes, but when he spoke again, it proved his mind was running along similar lines. "Have you ever thought of having kids?"

"I used to." She shrugged. "When I was younger. Even though I accepted I couldn't be the rebel I wanted to be, I still dreamed of a normal life. You know, marriage, kids."

"But now?"

"Now I'm more practical. Older. Don't get me wrong, spina bifida wouldn't keep me from having a family if I wanted one, but I'll be forty next year, and it takes a lot to maintain my health, my weight. I don't know if I would have the energy or ability in my forties to push a kid in a stroller or lug one around the way Jonnie does."

Their conversation turned then to friends, her college years, his interest in ancient civilizations and documentaries, where they had traveled, and places they still wanted to go. She admired the Montreal skyline but was glad they were there outside rush hour. In Pipeline she stretched her legs, then slept until they reached the US border crossing at Alexandria Bay where snow covered the ground in a thick layer, and she needed her crutches to access the rest area.

"Sorry I wasn't much company," she said when they were on the road again.

"No problem." He winked and patted her thigh. "But I had to turn the radio on, or your snoring would have put me to sleep, too."

"I snore?"

"Yes, ma'am."

"A quiet, ladylike snore?"

One could only hope. Yet she wasn't surprised when he shook his head. Oh well, just another example of her being womanly instead of ladylike.

"What about me? What do I do?"

"You burp," she said without hesitation.

"I do?"

"Not after snacks, but after every meal."

"Then I guess we're even. If you can put up with my burping—which is a compliment to the chef, by the way—I'll live with your snoring."

"Deal."

An hour later they passed Oneida Lake, and half an hour after that, he parked the car in front of Upstate University Medical Center. "Looks more like an airport than a hospital," he observed. The roof running along the side of the building where they sat resembled architecture found at drop-off terminals. "Do you want your crutches or your wheelchair?"

"Wheelchair."

The walkway was clear of snow and ice. Once her chair was unfolded and set up, she rolled toward the main entrance while he moved the car to the parking garage. Instead of going inside and registering, as she would have done had Hazel brought her, she sat outside and waited for him. Watched as he crossed the bridge back to the hospital and marveled at her good fortune.

What else could it be?

Of all the men in Somerset, he'd just happened to register his vehicles that particular Saturday when she just happened to be working. She might have gone another two years without meeting him. Might never have known the sound of his voice. The easy smile he shared with friends and strangers alike. His strong, square hands, his quick reflexes on the ice, his blue, blue eyes. Roger Plankey blue.

Through the glass panes of the sky bridge, she tracked his progress and thanked God for bringing him into her life, then went inside to meet him.

He wore his nice canvas coat, his Canadiens hat, and an Irish fisherman's sweater over olive wool pants. Those pants gave new definition to the word sexy. They weren't tight, but each time he moved, they highlighted his trim waist and muscular thighs.

"Ready to go?"

She nodded to the front desk behind her. "We have to check in first."

He accompanied her to the short waiting line. The first person finished, and he stepped closer to her so the woman could get by. Before moving away, he leaned down and whispered, "Don't think I missed you checking me out."

"It's your fault," she whispered back. "You're too handsome for your own good."

"Next."

They handed over their driver's licenses, provided appointment information, and left with color-coded day passes.

After routine tests, they left for the physicians' offices a quarter mile away. Lisa told him she wanted to use her wheelchair to get there.

"Are you sure? Because I can get the car if you'd rather ride."

"No, I like showing you off to the world."

"You say the sweetest things."

"I also like the fresh air. The snow."

"Well, they seem to have plenty of it already."

In fact, several inches were piled up next to the sidewalk, but she didn't mind. After being cooped up in the car for hours, despite their frequent breaks, she was enjoying the brisk air. She could feel it adding color to her cheeks.

No doubt that color was missing when she came out of her appointment at six o'clock. She was a blubbering mess. Despite cleaning up in the restroom, she couldn't hide her red eyes. Other women would duck out of the building or walk ahead of him, put physical distance between them in any number of ways, but those options were closed to her because she sat in her wheelchair. She didn't even have a hat or sunglasses to hide behind.

Instead of asking what was wrong, he merely folded the newspaper in his hand, dropped it on the waiting-room table, and came to his feet. "Ready to go?"

She fell in love with him right there.

Chapter Eleven

Her perfect man, keeping pace beside her, stepping forward to open the car door when they reached the parking garage. All without a word.

He took care of her wheelchair while she got into the passenger seat.

The windows fogged up from their breathing, and he let the engine run, the heater on, while the glass cleared. She snapped her seat belt on, and the sound of the buckle locking was loud in the taut silence.

"Do you want to talk?" he finally asked.

Yes. She wanted to share everything with him.

No. The doctor's recommendations pointed out what a freak she was, and she was afraid he would look at her differently once he heard them.

"Maybe when we're at the hotel?" he suggested when she said nothing.

A nod was the best she could do. He drove out of the garage, and she rested her cheek on the cold windowpane while years of hurt and disappointment swelled inside her chest.

She just wanted, for once, to be spontaneous. To have something special in her life that wasn't scripted, scheduled, or pre-planned.

"Wheelchair or crutches?" he asked when they were parked in front of the hotel lobby.

"Crutches."

"Room service, dining room, or go out for dinner?" he inquired when they were standing in their room with its two queen-sized beds.

"Dining room." Like a normal couple.

"Appetizers?" He raised his eyebrows above the menu in his hands.

"Just dinner." Because she was tired and a little heartsore.

"Are you going to talk to me tonight or force me to drag every word out of you?"

She put her menu down. Looked at him, waiting patiently on the other side of the table for her to direct the conversation, and wondered what to say.

He pushed the centerpiece aside and stretched his hands across the space between them. Palms open, an invitation, and she clasped his fingers like the lifeline they were.

"You've always been a straight shooter, darling. It's one of the things I love about you. Don't dissemble now."

He loved things about her? Did that mean he loved her?

The waiter approached, and she took her hands back.

"I'll tell you later. Promise." Because, despite their intimate table for two away from other diners, she felt too exposed to have this conversation here. "Let's just enjoy our dinner for now."

His surf-and-turf meal was delicious, if his after-dinner burp really was a compliment, and she even managed to appreciate her poached lobster salad, but as soon as they entered the hotel room, her worries returned, and she escaped to the lavatory.

It was time to go anyway, but she used it as a delaying tactic because she really didn't want to talk about her doctor's visit.

When she finally cracked the door open, two glasses sat on the nightstand between the queen-sized beds, a bottle of wine airing beside them. Roger's hiking boots were lined up parallel with the edge of one bed, and he had already turned down the covers. His hat hung from a headboard post.

He waited for her to sit on the opposite bed, facing him, before sitting down himself.

"So tell me, what was so bad that you lost your shine today?"

"My shine?"

"Darling, you shine like a string of Christmas tree lights. Bright. Colorful. Happy. I hate seeing that light dim. Tell me what's going on."

Flattered, she nonetheless took a fortifying breath before speaking. "I'm not really sure what you see in me. Okay, scratch that. It sounded pathetic, and this isn't about self-pity. But I'm disabled, and you're about as able-bodied as a man can get."

He grinned, and she couldn't resist poking him in the ribs with a nail, pumpkin orange with sprays of gold on the tips.

"Pay attention here."

"Yes, ma'am." A devilish glint in his blue eyes, he prompted, "You were saying something about my body?"

"Right." She scooted back on her bed to put more space between them. "Where do you think this is leading?"

"Am I supposed to have it all mapped out?"

"No, but you must have given it some thought."

"What I thought was that you seemed fun, and I wanted to know more about you." He reached across the gap between them, slid his hands beneath her thighs, and scooped her up into his arms. Sat down on his bed still holding her. Nuzzled her nose with his and stared into her eyes. "And I like everything I've learned so far."

A sigh gusted out of her lungs. She wanted to relax in his embrace and stop worrying about this, but he was right; she didn't hide from problems or confrontations. "So you're okay with me not being able to help with any chores? You wouldn't like it if I could walk around the farm with you in the evening?"

He grasped her chin between his thumb and forefinger. Kissed her softly on the cheek and nuzzled her ear. "I work all day, Lisa. Physical labor. When my day is over, I want to relax. A glass of wine, a good book, maybe a documentary program."

She knew this about him already.

"And I like your company. I'd love nothing more than to see you across the room working on your costumes while I'm reading a book. Or making new pieces of jewelry while I'm watching public television."

She could tell that he meant it, and the lump in her throat strangled her next words to a mere whisper. "You forgot about the wine."

"Ah, yes." Stretching his arm, he retrieved the bottle and glasses from the nightstand, then poured an inch of dark red liquid into each glass before putting the bottle back. "I like full-bodied reds like this one."

She took a sip, letting the wine coat her throat and warm her insides with its dark fruity flavors. "Hmm, it's good."

"Want to know the name?"

At her nod, his voice and smile turned wicked. "Burning Desire."

A laugh burst free from her tight chest, easing the pressure that had been building there.

"That's more like it." He grinned. "Now tell me what upset you so we can get through it together."

That lump in her throat returned. Her next word came out sounding like her mouth was filled with marbles. "Sex."

"Sex," he repeated.

"Yes, you know, the act between a man and—oh!" She shrieked when he tickled her underarm, and she almost lost her glass of wine.

"Serves you right," he said, though he dropped his hand to her hip once more. "I do know what the word means, and I've even experienced it a few times. Why were you and the doc talking about sex?"

She ran a finger around the rim of her wineglass while her cheeks grew warm. "Awkward."

"It doesn't have to be. I mean, if two people are attracted to one another—"

This time it was him belting out a laugh when she jabbed his jaw with her fist.

"Okay, be serious here." She sat up straight and got it over with. "I wanted to know if there was anything special I should do before the two of us—two people who are attracted to one another—engage in anything intimate. Assuming you're interested?"

"Fish no further, woman. I'm lured and caught."

"Thank you." She took a moment to enjoy that flattery before continuing. "Anyway, my condition can change over time, new concerns develop, etcetera."

"And?"

"And there's a whole list of stuff." She waved to the paperwork sticking out of her purse where it sat on a chair beside the bathroom door. "Icky stuff like enemas and douches."

"I see."

Her tension escalated again while she waited for him to say more. When he didn't, she finally broke the silence. "Kind of kills the mood, doesn't it?"

Roger hated the hurt in her voice. The uncertainty.

He removed the glass from her hand and put it on the nightstand with his own. Lifted her chin with the knuckle of his index finger and waited for her to meet his gaze before speaking.

"I know you can't just listen to your body because it doesn't always send the right signals, but you can trust your instincts." He kissed her wine-stained lips. "And you can trust me."

"With my body?" As a joke it fell flat, her attempted smirk wobbling a little bit.

"With your body," he confirmed, kissing her again. "And with everything else."

It was the closest he had come to confessing his growing feelings for her, but the moment the words left his mouth, he knew what they meant. Not since Mindy had he felt this way about a woman. Not even then, if he was honest, because they'd been green kids, best friends since junior high, embarking on the adventure of life together. This had hit him like a bolt of lightning. There he'd been, carrying on with the business of living and satisfied with it until that day he walked into the town clerk's office. He hadn't known anything was missing until he saw her bright smile behind the service window.

"That can either be your Bible"—he nodded to her purse and the documents from the clinic—"or you can burn it."

"Will you sleep with me tonight?" A whisper of sound, so unlike his usual confident Lisa. "I mean, share the bed with me?"

He lay back on the pillows and rolled with her still in his arms until they lay side by side.

"I don't want you to think I'm fast or anything," she clarified, kicking off her clogs. They dropped to the carpet with muted thuds.

"Everything about this is fast." He hadn't meant to say it aloud, but he'd only met the woman a month ago.

"Does it scare you?"

The uncertainty in her gaze cut him to the quick.

"More like excites me," he said. Kissing her lips, her cheek, her neck, he added, "I mean, I should probably be worried about whether or not you leave the toilet seat up or hog the remote control, but we'll figure it out."

She did laugh then, the full-throated sound he loved, cut short when he pulled her earlobe between his teeth and laved the soft cartilage.

"Tell me more."

"Hmm. You'll probably leave half a cup of coffee in the pot." Shifting his weight to one side, he snagged the zipper of her pullover top and slowly worked it down the center of her torso.

"Or drink orange juice directly from the carton." He spread the sides of her shirt apart and kissed her bare shoulder.

"You might not understand how hard it is for a man to work all day and still look this good."

She muffled a laugh against his throat.

He flicked the front clasp on her bra and fingered the lacy fabric aside. "Maybe you'll ply me with alcohol just to skip foreplay." Dipping his head, he licked the tip of one pink nipple.

She groaned and clutched the nape of his neck.

"You'll probably complain that I don't listen to you when you talk about yourself and your day," she suggested, finally getting into the spirit of things.

He rubbed light circles on her belly and palmed her breast, laving the other one with his tongue. She slid her hands beneath the hem of his thick sweater and stroked his back. Soft hands. Warm hands. He shuddered in appreciation.

"More likely you'll complain about me drinking beer with the girls."

Grinning, he pulled her breast into his mouth and suckled.

She gasped, breath hoarse when she continued, "Or that I'm not home at night, too busy having fun and losing track of time."

He let her nipple pop free of his mouth and kissed the upper slope of her breast, giving her a chance to recover. "Such bad habits you have," he chided, only to convulse when she scored his back with her nails, then buried them in his back pockets and squeezed.

In retaliation he blazed a trail of kisses from her collarbone down to her navel. She squirmed and giggled. Another ticklish spot for him to remember.

"What shall I do with you, darling?"

"Whatever you want," was her guttural reply. "Just

don't stop now."

****

He was thinking about that comment Friday morning. Remembering how she'd rested against him, panting in the aftermath of an orgasm he proudly gave her. She had promised to follow up with Dr. French as soon as they returned to Somerset. "I'll get all my questions answered. Because if you're that good at warm-up exercises, I want the whole thing!"

The woman was too sexy for her own good.

"Hey, Rog, you have a visitor."

Lifting his head from the flush system's hydraulic valve, he stared blankly at his father. Everyone who came to the farm was either a friend or there on business. *Who could it—* He didn't even finish the thought before suspicion made him say, "It's not a blonde woman, is it?"

"No. Brunette." His father shrugged and held out his hand for the wrench. "I'll get this."

Roger passed him the tool and wiped his hand on a rag as he went down the alley to the barn doors. Through the glass panels he could see a woman in a wool peacoat and knit hat with an embroidered flower blossom on the side. Her face was sideways to him, so he didn't recognize her until he opened the door.

"Hazel." He could only think of one thing to bring her here. "Is Lisa okay?"

"She's fine." Her serious brow puckered, and she pulled her bottom lip between her teeth before letting it go to say, "I was hoping we could talk for a few minutes. Is this a good time?"

Farming didn't come with scheduled rest breaks, but his father was as capable as he was of getting the valve fixed, so he nodded and motioned toward the house. He didn't invite her in through the milk shed. Instead, he waved to the porch, to the front door used for company. "Would you like to go inside?"

"No."

Okay, then. She hadn't come for a getting-to-know-you talk.

"What can I do for you?"

"I'm worried about your relationship with my sister."

The hackles on the back of his neck rose. Rather than let himself get riled, he kicked at the ground with his boot while taking a deep breath in, then letting it out slowly. "What has you worried?"

"Look, it's not you. You seem decent enough."

"Thanks."

"No, I mean it." Apparently, she didn't realize backhanded compliments were insults because she plowed on. "I've heard good things about you and your family. But Lisa isn't used to dating. She hasn't had long relationships, not since her early twenties anyway, and I'm afraid she might be in over her head. I don't want to see her get hurt."

"Shouldn't you be telling her this?"

Hazel huffed out a breath as if everything she'd said so far was logical and he was too obtuse to understand. "I have, but she's stubborn. She doesn't always think about where things might lead. How she might get hurt."

Could this woman be any more presumptuous? "Why are you assuming she'll get hurt?"

Another huff. A shake of her head. "What else could happen? You can't tell me you're actually in this for the long haul."

"Come again?" If his temper boiled any hotter, she'd soon find out the three feet between them wasn't nearly far enough.

"I think I'm muddling this."

"You think?"

"And now you're mad at me."

"That would be an understatement."

Those words got through to her. She raised her palms in an apologetic manner and took a step away. Showing some intelligence at last. "Look, I'm sorry. I just don't want my sister getting her heart broken."

"Her disability doesn't reach that far up her spine."

She gasped, clearly affronted, but he didn't give her a chance to speak.

"That's what this is really about, isn't it? You think because she has a physical disability, one that keeps her from doing very few things, by the way, that she's unlikely to get, and keep, a man's affection? That's why you doubt I might want more than a good time with her. Because you can't imagine anyone sticking around."

"I love her. I only want what's best for her."

"On your terms."

"You don't understand."

"Yes, I think I do. Either you underestimate your sister and how special she is, or you're jealous because I might become more important in her life than you are."

Chapter Twelve

"Ow!" Lisa complained into the telephone as soon as Jonnie answered Monday afternoon. Normally, they would be at her house for a manicure, but she'd canceled to take advantage of a last-minute opening with Dr. French. "I didn't know it was going to hurt so much."

"Well, what did you expect?"

She swore she heard muffled laughter in Jonnie's voice. "Are you kidding me? Every romance novel I've ever read makes it sound like there's this brief uncomfortable moment followed by earth-shattering orgasm. Are you telling me they all lied?"

"Yes." Jonnie hooted out loud. "Every one of them."

"Well, I call bullshit."

"Lisa! What would Hazel say if she could hear you?"

"I don't think that's a swear since I didn't take the Lord's name in vain. Besides, there are more cows in this part of Vermont than people. It's just a descriptive term here."

"And that's a rationalization if I ever heard one. We don't have that many bulls."

"But seriously. How long do you think I'll have to put up with this?"

"Take a long bath, and you'll be fine tomorrow."

"Just imagine if I had been completely *intact.*" She shuddered because this was bad enough. "Did they lie about the rest of it, too?"

"The rest of what?"

"You know. The orgasms. Are they really better than what I can manage myself, or should I be prepared for disappointment?"

"If Roger knows what he's doing, they're at least ten times better."

The man had some seriously hidden talents, but she wasn't going to tell her friend about their foreplay in the hotel room, instead saying, "Phew. That's a relief. I'd hate to think I put myself through this for nothing."

Yet despite the long bath, she was still sore the next day.

Roger came into the office as she was leaving her cubicle for lunch.

"I'm here to steal the boss lady for a meal." He slid his arm around her waist and gave her a thorough kiss. "Hello, darling."

Cold air clung to his canvas coat, but his embrace warmed every part of her. Her "hi" was a little breathless. She cleared her throat and tried again. "They're serving open-faced turkey sandwiches today."

"I think I'll pass on that special." Clasping her hand in his, he opened the frosted door with the other. "Even if we are in a hospital and I could get immediate treatment for an allergic reaction, I'd rather not lose half my day for a sandwich."

"Good idea. I don't want to lose you."

"You say the sweetest things."

She didn't respond, instead concentrating on making this walk as normal as possible so he wouldn't notice her gait being off. She said hello to Gwyneth at the front desk and Mark from radiology as he wheeled a patient back to the outpatient waiting room. Exchanged greetings with others between her office and the cafeteria, so they didn't have a chance to talk again until they were seated at a table. In the center of the room again.

Roger opened his roast beef sandwich and squirted mustard on the bread from a foil packet. He spread the condiment with a knife and put the slices of bread back together before asking, "Are you okay?"

"Me? Sure." She cut her turkey sandwich into pieces and mixed the cranberry sauce with it so she would get a bite of the fruit with every forkful, wondering why the cafeteria thought serving it just days after the holiday was a good idea, though she wasn't about to complain.

Roger took a bite of his sandwich and opened his milk carton. "You were walking slow."

"Oh, that." She waved her hand to indicate it was nothing to worry about. "I went to see the doctor yesterday."

"Routine appointment?"

Checking that no one could overhear them, she leaned forward on her elbows and explained. "No, I went to ask her those questions about intercourse since I'm planning to have it. With you." She winked. "In case you're wondering."

He preened like a peacock, sitting up straight and blowing on his knuckles before polishing them on his shoulder.

Dropping her voice even lower, she continued. Best to get this over with before she lost her nerve.

Being in a public place gave her courage she might not otherwise find. "The thing is, I've never had it before."

He raised his eyebrows for her to go on. Obviously not understanding what she was saying. Who would expect it from a thirty-nine-year-old woman?

"I'm not sure how much I'll feel down there, but if it's nothing and I only have this one time, I don't want it to hurt. So I saw the doc yesterday and asked her to pop that cherry."

He had her outside the cafeteria in sixty seconds flat. As soon as he stopped choking on his meal. After she reassured everyone in the vicinity that he was okay, just had something *go down the wrong way* while she thumped him on the back and alternately rubbed circles between his shoulder blades.

"A private place?"

Despite her bravado a few minutes ago, her voice squeaked from nerves when she replied, "Third door on the left."

It was a lactation room for nursing mothers to express milk. He propelled her inside and flipped the lock on the door handle. When he turned, his expression was as severe as his voice had been.

"Now, Roger," she began, crossing the room to put the coffee table between them. Hands raised in supplication. "I wanted to tell you, but I—"

The rest of her words were lost in a shriek of laughter as he all but tossed the coffee table aside and grabbed her around the middle.

"Didn't know how?" he guessed the rest of her sentence. "Maybe you thought it could wait until we spend the night together?"

"Don't get upset." She patted his shoulders and

couldn't help but smile. Even frustrated, stunned, maybe angry, the man was so handsome she wanted to touch him all over. "I want everything to be perfect."

He shut her up with a kiss. Not just any kiss. A long, long, long kiss that made her toes curl and all her feminine parts sizzle with heat.

"Was that perfect?" he asked when he finally let her up, gasping for breath.

She simply nodded because words escaped her.

He buried his face in the front of her sweater, sucking her breasts into his mouth, fabric and all. His hands shaped her back, her bottom, pulling her into his body while she quivered from head to toe.

"And that? How was that?"

The most she could manage was a moan.

Pressing his forehead to hers, he walked her backward until she rested against the wall. His kiss this time was soft and sweet but no less potent than the others. "Why didn't you tell me when we were in New York?"

She shrugged, embarrassed despite her tough-woman act.

"Lisa, look at me."

She hadn't realized she wasn't, but now she lifted her gaze from his collar to his face.

"I might have hurt you. In New York. If I'd had a latex-free condom on me..." His voice trailed off, and he hugged her to him. "Darling, the last thing I'd ever want to do is hurt you."

"You didn't," she assured him, wrapping her arms around his waist and resting her cheek on his shoulder. "It was perfect."

He pulled his head back to look at her with those

beautiful blue eyes. "Did it feel good?"

"You know it did."

"Then trust me to make the real thing even better."

"I can't imagine *that* being possible."

He grinned, shook his head, and kissed her soundly. "Then that gives you something to look forward to, doesn't it?"

****

In fact, he was looking forward to it himself. The boys had final exams in two weeks, and once they were home for Christmas break, he planned to spend the night at Lisa's house. Maybe more than one night. The outrageous woman owed him a few after pulling that stunt in the hospital cafeteria. His epitaph might have read *death by roast beef.* Not exactly how he wanted to be remembered when he breathed his last.

But he got a little of his own back when he presented her with a drawing later that night. She and the girls made Indian pudding with homemade whipped cream. He was sitting at her table with the three of them, enjoying the fruits of their labor, when Lisa opened the card he'd sketched that afternoon.

"It's you!" Darcy exclaimed, immediately recognizing the pretty little witch in the graveyard. She peered over Lisa's shoulder for a closer look. "I don't get it. The gravestone is for you, Uncle Roger?"

He nodded, licking the molasses and cornmeal dessert from his spoon as if it were any other day. Any other drawing.

"So what's that on the stone?"

Enjoying himself immensely, he grinned at Lisa's bright-red cheeks and sparkling hazel-green eyes and said, "Why, pumpkin, that's a cherry on top."

Lisa choked on her pudding.

****

"I think we're even," she declared when he parked at The Gables Thursday night. To make up for his lost lunch on Tuesday, she was treating him to dinner.

"Does that mean we'll get through an entire meal together with no surprises?" He wasn't keeping a scorecard, but he wouldn't mind having a quiet, romantic evening with her.

"Unless that blonde woman stuck around when the rest of the cast left last weekend."

"You'd better stay close just in case."

He helped her from the truck and ushered her into the lobby where a young woman at the hostess station offered them a smile of welcome. "Table for two?"

"We have reservations," Lisa said, "under Kirkpatrick."

The hostess looked at a diagram on the stand and marked one square with a pencil. "Would you like to leave your coats out here or take them with you?"

They hung them on pegs by the door, and he got his first glimpse of tonight's outfit. A fitted black shirt over black dress slacks. Subdued, for Lisa, until he looked closely at the print of the top. Those weren't roses decorating the background but cherries.

"Did you make that for me?"

She winked and took his hand, whispering, "Who else?"

He didn't reply because the hostess showed them into the dining room where two other parties were already seated, but he did whisper, "I owe you one," before they stopped at a four-top set for two in a corner by the fireplace. A giant Christmas tree glowed from the opposite corner, and evergreen garland hung in swags from the overhead chandelier. It was pretty, the music in the background quiet and soothing, the woman across the table from him glowing as warm as the fire in the grate.

"Olivia will be your server tonight," the hostess announced after reciting the dinner specials. "Can I start you off with something to drink?"

They ordered, then made small talk while perusing the menu.

"Looks a lot different here than when I came in July," he noted. "I like the holiday decorations."

"Hmm. Jonnie is good at decorating, but really this is all David."

"I'm surprised they don't use electronic order pads." On the few occasions he had met David Wang, the man seemed as modern a restaurateur as he was a farmer.

"David thinks waitstaff spend all their time staring at a screen instead of their customers if they use them." She selected a whole-grain breadstick from the lined basket and dipped it in a bowl of fancy goat cheese. "Hmm, this is delicious."

He split a hard roll in two and spread some of the dip on half. "It *is* good," he admitted after taking a bite, "even if the cheese doesn't come from a cow."

"Dairy snob."

"And proud of it."

They turned their attention back to the menus, ready to place their order when Olivia arrived with their drinks. She wrote it down, said, "I'll put that right in," and left them alone again.

That lasted about two minutes. No sooner had they

taken a sip of their spiced cider than Jonnie arrived in the doorway with her four little boys in tow.

"Sorry to bother you." She adjusted the roly-poly one at her hip while holding the oldest boy's hand. The other two climbed up into the empty chairs at their table as if they had been invited.

"They saw you in the parking lot and begged to see you before bedtime since we didn't get to come over Monday afternoon."

" 'Cause you had a doctor's appointment," Elijah supplied, and Roger ducked his head to keep from laughing.

Unfazed, Lisa took a breadstick from the basket, broke it into four pieces, and gave one to each boy.

"Know what I'm going to ask Santa to bring me for Christmas?" Malachi said apropos of nothing. His dark eyes glittered almost as brightly as the snowflakes dangling from Lisa's earlobes, and his little body vibrated with energy. Roger suspected he would need one of those wiggle cushions when he was old enough to attend school, or he would bounce off the walls and miss all his lessons.

Lisa leaned in close to him and whispered conspiratorially, "Tell me."

"A puppy!"

She reeled back in mock surprise. "No way."

"It's all he talks about," Jonnie said. "Ever since he saw a humane society ad on television. Then he met Sara's dog, Cortland, and now there's nothing else on his list."

"Just a dog," Malachi confirmed.

Lisa broke another breadstick, swirled the tip in the cheese, and offered it to Jonnie, who shuddered and backed away, bumping into her husband as he came into the room behind her.

He draped one arm over Jonnie's shoulder and stroked the baby's nose with his free hand. "Did you tell her your news?"

Roger noticed Jonnie was a little pale.

Lisa must have made the same observation. "Have you lost weight?" she asked, then caught her breath and, not giving her friend a chance to answer, said, "Please, don't tell me you're sick."

"Nope. Just pregnant."

Roger barely saved their table settings when Lisa jumped up to give Jonnie a hug and the tablecloth caught on her allergy bracelet.

"Don't you ever scare me like that again!" Lisa admonished, almost immediately adding, "Pregnant! Hallelujah. The one thing you two are missing in your lives is kids."

"Very funny. You do know who they're staying with if we ever go away for a romantic weekend, right?"

"You're never going away. Five kids? Seriously, if you go away, you'll end up with six."

"Fine by us."

Returning to her seat, relief clear on her face, Lisa said, "So tell me, crazy lady, when does this one make an appearance?"

"March fourteenth."

"Make it a month early. That way we can celebrate Valentine's Day in style."

"Would you like to be one of the three fairy godmothers?" David asked.

"Me? Three!" Her eyes glowed at the idea.

"You, Abby, and Emmeline." Jonnie grinned over her shoulder at her husband. "The *fairy* part was his idea. He said he wouldn't put it past you to make pastel capes with hoods for each of you to wear at the christening."

"Ha!" Lisa belted out her signature laugh. Full throttle and full of joy. "Count me in."

"Thank you."

Beside them, Malachi pouted. "Babies are stupid. That's why I want a dog."

A pained silence replaced the celebratory atmosphere.

Roger slung an arm over the back of the boy's chair, going for a nonchalant look so he wouldn't get suspicious. "You go to school yet?"

Malachi shook his head, as forlorn as a boy could be.

"Hmm. Probably not old enough for a job, then."

"I can work!" From down in the dumps to defensive.

"Any chance you're available two or three days a week, for half an hour or so?"

"That might be arranged," David answered for him.

"Well"—Roger bent low over the table and looked Malachi in the eye, man to man—"I have a dog, Sadie, and my little boy is away at college, so she doesn't get as much exercise as she needs to. Seems to me you might be just the right person for the job. That is if you're interested?"

Liquid dark eyes turned to his parents, full of hope and entreaty.

"It's a big responsibility," Jonnie cautioned, but her gaze was warm, and above the boy's head David mouthed, *thank you.*

"Whadya say you come over to my place and play with her so she doesn't get lonely and out of shape? That is if you think you can keep up with her. She's pretty active." He exchanged a grin with Lisa, because if anyone could keep up with Sadie, this boy could.

"Can I, Jonnie? Please?"

"If you're sure it wouldn't be any trouble?"

Roger waved away her concern. "What's one more boy on a farm?"

Chapter Thirteen

"Tell me you're not letting him go," Jonnie demanded as soon as she came into the house Monday afternoon for Lisa's weekly manicure.

"Not in this lifetime."

"Phew." She put Gideon down on the floor and took off his mittens and coat before upending a bucket of blocks for him to play with. "I left the other boys with David so we could talk."

"Uh-oh. The last time someone said that to me, it didn't end well."

Jonnie slid into a chair at the table opposite from her. "Hazel came to visit?"

"No, she asked me over for lunch after church."

"That must have been a fun time." Jonnie made a face, and Lisa couldn't blame her.

She and Hazel shared little beyond their DNA. Her sister was a good person, in fact she was a kind, gentle person with everyone else, but put the two of them together in a room, and it was like baking soda and vinegar. Eruptions guaranteed.

"She's worried about me."

"So what else is new? Isn't that a job description for her?"

"Ain't that the truth?" Lisa held up a coffee pod, eyebrows raised, but Jonnie shook her head, so she put it away. "No more caffeine?"

"Not until the little one arrives." She opened her manicure case. "I was thinking dark-blue base to snow-white tips with gradients of blue and silver in between. What do you say?"

"Perfect." Lisa removed the old nail polish while Jonnie set out her supplies. "I think my parents messed up with both of us," she admitted, "and I feel guilty saying that, because they were good parents. But they told me to be careful from the time I could walk, and they told Hazel to take care of me from the time she could talk."

"A burden for both of you."

"Hmm." Lisa didn't want to be mad at her little sister or resent her. She knew Hazel didn't want to be frustrated with her. Maybe they could find a reset button somewhere for their relationship. She shook that off for now. "So what did you want to talk about? My man or something else?"

"Your man, of course. Is he bringing you to the wedding tomorrow night?"

"Sure is." Her cheeks warmed as excitement coursed through her veins.

Jonnie stopped laying out her manicure equipment. "What is it?"

"He's spending the night!"

The answer burst out of her, the same way she had announced her first date with him back in October. Loud enough for them to hear her over in Morgan or up on Gore Mountain.

Gideon started to wail.

"Oh no."

Jonnie scooped him up off the floor and rocked him in her elbow, kissing his curly dark hair, his plump dark cheeks, his little button nose. All the while making those reassuring shushing noises mothers made. His sobbing turned into whimpers, those whimpers into hiccoughs, and when she swung around in circles, he chortled like the happy baby he had become under her regular care.

"Sorry about that." Lisa would never intentionally upset the little boy. He and his brothers were the closest thing to nephews she had, and she adored them.

"It's okay." Jonnie put him back down on the floor with his blocks but stayed with him until he was playing on his own again. "Now, tell me all about it."

"We were going to wait another week until Bryce and Colin are home on break and can help with the milking, but Glen has Wednesday off. It's Feast of the Immaculate Conception Day in Canada."

"Say what?"

"A Catholic holiday. Most businesses are still open, but so many of Glen's co-workers take the day off that he's going to work from home. Anyway, Roger asked if he wouldn't mind helping with the morning chores so we could have some *alone time.* I guess the twins still get up in the middle of the night, so Glen said he'd be awake already and it'd be no big deal."

"Maybe not to him."

"No kidding. Half the time I think there's no way I'll sleep between now and then. The other half I feel like I'm going to pass out from nerves."

****

She was still pumped full of that crazy adrenaline mix when he picked her up the following evening. Literally picked her up so the hem of her palazzo pants wouldn't get wet in the falling snow accumulating in her driveway.

"I can walk," she objected, only to clutch at his shoulders when he pretended to stagger beneath her weight and almost drop her. "That was not very nice of you."

"Just a little payback." He opened the truck cab and put her down on the seat. Leaned in and brushed a kiss across her lips. "Did you hear me complaining?"

"No. But I'm not completely helpless."

His head reared back at that comment. "I'm sorry. I don't mean to treat you that way."

She wrapped her hand around his neck and pulled him down, kissing him until they were both breathing hard. "No one has every treated me more like an able-bodied woman than you."

"And what a body it is."

Pushing at his shoulder, she scoffed. "Better get in before we're late for the wedding."

"Do you want your wheelchair or crutches?"

"Neither." She raised her right pants leg to reveal a brace wrapped around her ankle and calf. "Good old-fashioned orthotics. These are my dancing feet."

He laughed and shut the door.

When he slid into the driver's seat, his fresh, manly scent filled the cab. Droplets of water clung to the ends of his dark hair.

"Just get out of the shower?"

"Quickest one I've ever taken."

He looked both ways at the end of the drive, and she noticed his Canadiens cap. Under cover of the seat, she crossed her fingers and said a quick prayer for luck because the hospital auxiliary fundraiser drawing was this week, and she had put all her 50/50 prize money on chances to win game tickets for him.

"At least the wedding's odd timing doesn't get in the way of your chores."

"Hmm. Emmeline said they met on a Tuesday night."

"That explains it, then. She's one of the most down-to-earth, practical nurses on our staff, so I wondered."

"She's sentimental, though. And you know what they say; love makes people do crazy things."

She bit her lip to keep her own crazy from spilling out. She liked to think she was a practical woman, too, despite her flair for costumes and celebrations, but telling him she was falling in love with him after only six weeks might send him running.

"Oh, good. Looks like Emmeline's grandparents made it after all."

The Gables parking lot was filled with cars. A combination of mostly Vermont and New York plates with a blue-and-white Quebec plate added to the mix. He nodded to the last. "I haven't seen them since they left the Townships. Fifteen years ago, at least. They used to host the family reunions before that."

"You like them?"

"They're good people. Maman told me he doesn't see well now, but I'm glad they could make it. For Emmeline." He retrieved a flat package from behind the seat and handed it to her. "Can you take this for me while I help you out?"

She held it to her chest with one hand and, when he came around to open her door, wrapped the other one around his shoulder. Sliding into his hold like she belonged there. God, it felt good to be wanted. To have someone this familiar with her who kept coming back for more. Despite her assertion of independence earlier, she snuggled against him while he carried her to the roofed entry and set her down on the welcome mat.

"I'm going to park the truck at the back of the lot. Why don't you go on in?"

"Or I can wait here for you."

He gave her a hard kiss. "Or you can wait here for me."

Crossing the lot a couple of minutes later, Roger marveled at fate, luck, or whatever it was that brought the two of them together.

He wasn't a proud man. Watching helplessly while Mindy lost her battle with cancer pretty much buried any ego he might have had when he was younger. Yet seeing Lisa standing beneath the entry lights, her brown curls peeking out beneath a white knit toque and her big hazel eyes tracking his movements as he came closer, he felt something very close to pride. Or maybe it was honor. Of all the single men in Somerset, and there were plenty of them, she chose to be with him.

"Hiya, handsome. Can I interest you in a party?"

"Every day of the week and twice on Sundays as long as you're my partner."

"You're a charmer, Mr. Farmer."

"You're pretty cute yourself." He reached past her and opened the door, letting her cross the threshold ahead of him.

Inside they were greeted by sounds of revelry from the function room at the back of the lobby. Behind the batwing doors to their left, the kitchen lights were on, but the dining room to their right was dark, a rolling garment rack barring the entry to it.

He added his coat and gloves to the items already stored there, then took the wedding gift from her so she could remove her outer gear.

"Wow." Beneath a snowy-white capelet edged with blue-and-silver gemstones, a dark-blue pantsuit hugged her curves—her breasts, the indentation of her waist, the flare of her hips. Wide vintage-style legs only accented the womanly form above them. "Can we just turn around and go home now?" he whispered at her ear. "I've suddenly got the urge to have you all to myself."

"Hey, Pop."

"Damn. Foiled again." Sliding his arm around Lisa's waist, he turned to his son. "Hey, Trev, Amy, I'd like you to meet my friend. Lisa, this is my oldest son and his fiancée."

That was the first of many introductions. His cousin Emmeline was marrying David's brother, Romney, so Lisa knew most of the groom's family, and he knew all of Emmeline's guests.

He finally asked her to dance as an excuse to have her to himself.

"A slow song." Wrapping her hands around his middle, she rested her cheek against his shoulder. "Good choice."

Although he couldn't take credit for choosing the number, he wasn't about to complain.

Everything about this felt right. From the moment he met her, just six weeks ago, something had sparked to life inside him that had lain dormant for almost two decades. Like he had found a puzzle piece he hadn't known was missing in the first place.

This pretty, vivacious woman fit right into his life.

When the song ended and Jonnie peeled her away from him, he almost didn't know what to do with himself.

"You two are getting pretty chummy." His sister, Linda, approached with a mug of beer in hand. "No drink?"

"I had a glass of wine, but I'm driving."

She took a swallow of the yellow lager, licked foam from her top lip, and returned to her earlier statement. "Is this leading somewhere?"

Normally he would shrug and tell her to mind her own business. But as he gazed across the room to where Lisa crouched down in front of Jonnie's two oldest boys, her eyes wide as if what they had to tell her were the secrets to the universe, he didn't even think twice. "Yes. It's leading somewhere."

"Good for you. She seems like a lot of fun."

Lisa returned to his side then, the dark-blue fabric of her outfit molding to her pear-shaped figure, and all he could think about was the fun they were going to have when they got back to her house.

"Everybody on the dance floor!" someone yelled from the mic on the corner stage.

Jimmy Duncan grabbed his sister's hand. Feet stomped. Hands clapped. Glassware shook on the tables as a rowdy country tune began.

"Shall we join them?"

"Absolutely."

They danced to that song and one more before returning to chairs along the wall. He wasn't sure how much she could handle without getting tired, and he thought he saw her stumble once on the last number, so he used thirst as an excuse to take a break.

Sitting probably wasn't the best idea, though. Half an hour later he was yawning wide enough to crack his jaw.

"I think I'd better get you home," Lisa remarked when he covered his mouth for the third time in less than five minutes. "It's been a while since four a.m."

"Sorry about that."

"Don't apologize. I'm being selfish." Leaning close, she husked, "I want to make sure you still have some energy left over for me tonight."

Suddenly revitalized, he dug the truck keys out of his pants pocket and dangled them in front of her face. "Check, please."

She nipped his ear with her teeth. "We should probably say goodbye to the bride and groom first."

"Okay. But let's hurry."

They found Romney and Emmeline in another dining room, opening gifts. "A lot of our guests have to fly out tomorrow, and we wanted to thank them in person before they go," Emmeline explained, setting aside the notebook where she was recording what they received and from whom. "What does your present look like?"

"It's the flat silver one." Roger motioned to where it sat atop a large multicolored box. "But you don't have to open it on my account."

"Of course, she does." This from Romney, who handed the gift to her, then took up the notebook and pen.

Roger wasn't generous with tape, so it only took a couple flicks of Emmeline's fingernail before she peeled back the paper and revealed a clear plastic bag filled with embroidered white cotton. "A tablecloth?"

"Pillowcases."

"Oh. Thank you."

"Your mother made them for me and Mindy when we got married. Mindy would never use them because she was afraid she'd get them dirty and not be able to get the stains out. They've been in a cedar chest all these years. I thought you might like to have something from your mom on your wedding day."

Chapter Fourteen

"Way to make an impression," Lisa said when they were descending the S curves on their way into town. "Did you know she'd cry?"

"No, but I'm not really surprised. Emmeline has always been sensitive, and she was a mommy's girl. She was only ten when the car accident happened. It was tough on her."

"You like her." Lisa did, too, but outside of the surgical unit, Emmeline could be aloof with people, and not everyone saw past her protective shell.

"She's a good kid." He stopped at the bottom of Gore Mountain Road and checked for traffic before turning right onto Circle Row. The roads were a little greasy, the back end of the truck swinging a foot or two over the invisible center line before he got it back into their lane. "They seem like a good match, her and Romney."

"I think you got his stamp of approval."

In fact, the groom had effusively thanked him for making Emmeline cry on their wedding day. "Those are happy tears," he'd insisted when Roger apologized. "Maybe not now, but she'll cherish those forever. You couldn't have given her a better gift."

Roger made a wide turn onto one of the side roads leading up to the common. Ahead of them the dim glow of antique streetlamps marked the oval while fairy lights strung through the maple trees illuminated the steadily falling snow.

No other cars were on the road. Roger took his half out of the middle, chasing his headlights around the common until they reached Pleasant Street where he slowed to avoid another slide before making that turn.

The rumble of the diesel engine faded to background noise as they climbed the hill to Somerset Place. The beating of her heart grew loud in her ears. Blood rushed to parts of her body that had been relaxed, making them heavy and full.

She was thirty-nine years old and bringing a man home for the first time.

A plow truck lumbered down the hill from the hospital. When it passed the entrance to her development, the American flag on the lighted pole caught in the vehicle's slipstream and snapped so loudly she jumped in her seat.

Roger reached across the cab and squeezed her knee. "You okay, darling?"

"Yes." Excited. Nervous. Juggling equal parts fear and expectation. "I'm fine."

"Hmm." A non-reply.

Neither one of them said anything else until they were inside her house removing their winter wear.

"I bought you a toothbrush."

As a romantic opener, it lacked charm, but he smiled and lined his boots up on the mat beside her front door while she sat on the deacon's bench and lifted her pants legs to get at her own shoes. Clunky, ugly things, but they fit over her orthotics, and wearing them meant she could dance without losing her balance.

"Do those help? I mean, do they help you stay on

your feet?"

"Yeah. When I want to do more than just walk, they help keep me steady."

He knelt before her and unbuckled the shoe opposite the one she worked on. "Have you always had them?"

She shrugged, realized he couldn't see her reaction, and said, "Losing my toe cost me more than my pride. I've had to use them more since then because it threw off my balance."

He took the shoe from her hand and placed both on the rubber mat beside his boots. When she bent over to start on her AFOs, he brushed her hand aside. "Let me."

Not sure why he wanted to, she nonetheless sat back and watched as he ripped the Velcro straps free, then slid the hard orthotic shell from her foot, ankle, and calf. She flexed her toes and watched while he removed the other one.

Bracing her hands on either side of the bench, she made to stand, but again he stopped her, this time with a palm against her belly. "Wait."

"What for?"

He didn't reply. Instead, he lifted her right foot onto his thigh and slid his hands up her calf to her knee. Took the top edge of her stocking between his fingers and rolled it down the length of her leg. Lifted her foot enough to remove the hosiery completely, then folded it and put it inside her shoe.

Small indentations from the brace marked her calves. He smoothed his fingers over those depressions, then knocked the breath from her lungs when he leaned forward and kissed them.

Her head hit the wall. Desire gripped her insides

until she was afraid to move, panting softly while her hands floundered helplessly on the bench.

"Your skin is so soft," he murmured, kissing the inside of her knee while his hand massaged the sole of her foot. She jerked reflexively. Her limbs shook with the effort of holding still while warmth suffused other body parts.

He placed her foot on his thigh and took the other in his hands. "On our first date you wore black booties, and I noticed how little your feet are." He rolled the stocking down that leg, removed it, and folded it up like he had its mate. "I thought they were so cute."

She didn't want him seeing her that way, unless he was talking about her behavior.

As if she gave voice to that thought, he continued. "But when you joined me in the hot tub? Hot damn." Leaning forward, he kissed the indentations on her leg. "Nothing *cute* about this body. You're all woman."

He was lighting her up like a switchboard. Nerve endings that didn't always fire on all cylinders had no trouble processing each sensation as he kissed and stroked and laved her skin. Perspiration dotted her upper lip. She rolled her head back and forth against the wall behind her.

He trailed his fingers down one leg and grasped her hip with the other, pulling her gently to the edge of the bench. Their gazes locked. In his she saw the same heat now rolling through her body. A heat that magnified when he came to his feet, lifting her to stand and wrapping his arms around her.

He kissed her forehead, her cheek, the side of her neck.

"I've been watching you in this outfit all night," he

173

murmured, his warm breath at her ear making her shudder. "It's beautiful. You're beautiful."

He swirled his tongue over her earlobe, and she convulsed against him.

"And all I want to do is see you out of it."

She moaned at the heady compliment, and he caught the sound with his kiss. A hot, deep kiss that made her rise on tiptoes while her insides quivered with longing.

"Tell me you want the same thing," he growled.

"Umm, duh?" she whispered shakily.

His chuckle went through her like a bass drum. Low and deep and reverberating long after the sound ended, making everything heavy—her core, her breasts, even her eyelids.

He lifted her off the floor and placed her feet on his like that day at the ice rink. Not letting go, he kissed her while walking backward into her bedroom. When they reached the edge of the bed, he sank down onto the comforter, holding her to him with one hand while the other slid up her side to cup her breast. She mewled with pleasure, and when his thumb flicked her nipple, a quiver ran straight through to her core.

"I've got to use the restroom," she gasped.

She had been so caught up in the moment, so lost to his lovemaking, she'd forgotten who she was. If she didn't use a quick catheter, she could end up making a mess of their first time together. No way did she want to risk that! She finally had the man right where she wanted him.

"Promise you won't move."

"That might prove difficult, darling."

She was wrapped around him, arms and legs

meeting at his back, his head nestled in the crook of her neck and shoulder while his palms did wonderful things for her body temperature.

"Say it again," she breathed, rocking back and forth against him.

"Say what, darling?"

A groan of longing, of belonging, rippled through her.

"That's it." With an impatient hug, she unraveled her limbs before she could get lost in his lovemaking again and pushed at his chest. He let his hands fall away from her. Offered one to help her up from the bed when she struggled to her feet.

"Don't you dare touch me now." Sidestepping him, she wobbled her way to the bathroom. Not off-balance but dizzy from lust. "I'll only be a minute."

Or five. Excited she might be, but she had needs to see to, makeup to remove, and a sexy piece of nightwear to slither into.

Her first time! With a man she was certain was her future, her true love, her...everything. So perfect for her that if she had written out a list of requirements, he would have ticked off every box. Even the burping after meals and the little patch of skin on the crown of his head were perfect. He was her kind of steady. Her kind of crazy.

"Lisa?"

His voice through the door made her insides clench. "I'll be right out." Her reply was more of a high squeak than a sentence.

She was clearing her throat to try again when he said, "Are you okay, darling?"

That did it. Out of nowhere, tears flooded her eyes

so she could barely see to grab her robe from the hook by the shower. She managed to get it on and haphazardly tie the sash before opening the door. An inch. Just enough to see him leaning against the wall beside it. Blue gaze steady on her face. Waiting for her to make the next move. To chicken out or soldier on.

"Second thoughts?"

His mother's accent slipped into his speech. He hadn't said *are you okay* as much as *ehr you okay?* And now he said *segond* instead of second. Proof he had as much at stake here as she did. Restoring her equilibrium as nothing else could have.

She toed the door open a few more inches and slipped her hand into his. "Not a one. Just a little nervous." Squeezing his fingers, she stepped back and motioned to the bathroom. "Do you need to use it?"

"Don't mind if I do."

As soon as the door closed behind him, she scooped Mischief off the bed and set him down in the hall outside the bedroom. "Sorry, pal," she said in response to his disgruntled hiss. *Sorry, not sorry.* Lazy he might be, but he was also curious, and the last thing she needed was him snuggling between them in the middle of lovemaking. With one apologetic stroke to his head, she closed the door and shut him out.

Now what?

Turn off the overhead light, turn on the bedside lamps. Better. Muted. Romantic.

Should she get under the covers? Stand here waiting? Take off her robe? Leave it on?

****

Roger wasn't surprised to find her paralyzed by indecision when he stepped out of the bathroom. Any woman would be, facing her first time, but he was determined to give her a night she'd never forget.

"Keep pacing, and you'll make me nervous," he said to put her at ease. If the way she fell into his embrace was any indication, it worked.

"Sorry about that."

"No apologies." He kissed the top of her head, her forehead, her lips. Took the tie of her robe and started to undo it, but she pressed a hand over his fingers and stopped him.

Maybe she would feel less vulnerable if he was half naked instead of fully dressed. Stepping back, he pulled his shirt off and tossed it onto the bench at the foot of her bed.

Her wide eyes made a slow study of his bare torso, so he flexed his biceps and rippled his abs for her. "Like what you see?"

"And then some."

Her fingers sifted through the hair bisecting his chest before she wrapped them around his neck and devastated him with a kiss. Could the woman kiss! By the time they came up for air, he was so hard he had to unsnap his jeans to get some relief.

"Can I help you off with your robe now?"

A blush stained her cheeks. Her hazel eyes darted away from him.

"What have you been up to, darling?" He was a little bit suspicious but mostly curious because she was full of surprises.

"Nothing."

He couldn't tell if her high squeak was from laughter or embarrassment, so he sat up against the headboard and waited. Like he didn't mind being physically separated from her. Like he could wait all night. "Show me."

Blushing even brighter than she had before, she sat on the edge of the bed and untied her robe, pulling it off her shoulders. Revealing a white satin gown edged in black lace and covered with some sort of black-and-red design. He didn't understand why that would make her self-conscious. The slip fell to mid-thigh and covered more than her swimsuit had. Then he looked closer and realized the print was embroidered text. Above her left breast he read *Napoleon was once attacked by a horde of bunnies.*

Beneath her arm, *Mary really had a little lamb, and it followed her to school in Boston.*

Similar lines covered the length of the gown.

"Did you make this for me?"

She dropped the robe to the floor and lay down beside him. "Well, you love ancient history, and I didn't want you to get bored."

As if that could ever happen. "How very...thoughtful of you. But maybe it should be in braille?" To prove how useful that would be, he ran his fingers along the next line. *In ancient Greece the unibrow was a sign of intelligence and great beauty.*

Her breath stuttered.

"Not bothering you, is it?" he teased, moving on to the writing directly over her right nipple. She froze when his finger traced the long sentence, written in a circular swirl so that it ended on the point which was now noticeably hard. *Mayans would dangle items between their children's eyes, hoping to make them cross-eyed.*

He jerked back. "What?"

"I guess it meant they were favored by the sun or something," she explained, her voice a mere croak, "if they had crossed eyes."

She shifted her legs, her small feet digging into the sheet beneath them. Arousal in every movement, each sigh of breath, the dew on her upper lip.

"I may have read that one wrong." His own voice had some gravel in it, but his fingers were working just fine. He ran them over the embroidered script again while he closed his other hand over her hip. Holding her still. Holding her to him.

A breath hissed out of her when he reached the end of the sentence again.

He caught the edge of the gown with one finger and pulled it down until it caught on her nipple, serving it up to him like an appetizer before the feast. And he was a hungry man.

Still holding her hip with one hand, he rolled over and propped himself up with the opposite elbow so he wouldn't crush her, dropped his head, and licked the pretty pink bud.

The breath gusted out of her. Taking that as a compliment, he laved the nipple again and slid his hand up the length of her satin slip until he could cup her other breast. He ran his thumb over that nipple at the same time he suckled on its twin.

She groaned and arched her neck, thighs naturally falling open, then closing around his hips and drawing him in.

He bit down gently on her nipple, and she lurched halfway up into a sitting position. Eyes wide open but glazed, lips parted on a gasp.

"Touch me," he urged. Because if she didn't put

her hands on him soon, he might die.

With a little mewl, she reached for him. Scraped her nails through his hair and rubbed the bald spot on the back of his head. A sizzle ran down his spine. His pants were so tight he ground himself against her for relief. She wrapped her legs around his back and pulled him closer.

Her hands were everywhere now. Grasping whatever she could touch, holding him tight while she writhed beneath his attentions.

He caught the hem of her gown and slid the satin up until his hand touched nothing but warm flesh. She fell still beneath him. Until his fingers danced their way across her hip and brushed the soft hair protecting her core. Then she started to shake, so hard she almost dragged her breast from his mouth. He let it go with a pop. Captured her lips with his own while his fingers explored their destination.

She slid her hands inside the back of his jeans and palmed his buttocks. He arched his back, thumbed her clitoris, and their mouths clashed in carnal desperation.

Chapter Fifteen

Lisa decided breathing was highly overrated. It had always seemed important in the past, but if she died of asphyxiation from this kiss, her tombstone would be covered with happy faces.

Nothing in the privacy of her bedroom prepared her for this. For him.

He seemed to know exactly what she needed. The heavy pool of lust weighing her down was lifted by his fingers. Magic fingers, touching, probing, stroking, urging her to rock against him. She had taken care of her own needs before but always wondered if she had full sensation. He left her without any doubt.

Everything inside her rose to this occasion. Almost as if her nerves had lain dormant before his touch. When he slid one finger inside her, she gripped his shoulders. When a second finger joined the first, she pulled her mouth away from his and gasped. Apparently, she needed oxygen after all. But when those fingers slid in and out of her body, she bit down on his shoulder to stifle a scream.

He thumbed her clit again, and she convulsed against him. A long slow ripple of yearning seized her insides. When he rubbed circles on the tiny nerve center, the ripple turned into a tremor. Chills rushed down her arms.

She kissed his shoulder, licked his neck, bit his

earlobe. Held on for dear life when his fingers crooked inside her and her body seized up, then liquefied.

"That's my gal." Nuzzling her cheek, he rolled onto his side with her still wrapped in his arms. His body was tense, his voice husky. "There's something in my pocket for you."

Though he lifted his hips and twisted to give her better access, she couldn't even work her fingers inside. "I'm flattered." Because she was responsible for that bulge.

His laugh was a painful sound.

"Let me relieve some of that pressure."

Easier said than done. The zipper on his jeans was stretched so taut it wouldn't give when she tried pulling the tab down.

After several attempts he tried to assist her. She swatted his fingers away and defiantly straddled his thighs. "I've got this."

"Oh, darling." He chuckled. "I'm not sure that's going to help much—"

Anything else he planned to say was lost when she cupped him through the denim with one hand, holding him still and forcing the material on either side of the fly together while she worked the zipper free with her other hand.

He spilled out into her palm.

"Well, hello to you, too." She grinned.

Roger groaned and reached for her hips. Again, she batted his hands away, this time levering herself up above him so she could work the jeans and boxers down his thighs. Determined to do this on her own, though she didn't object when he lifted his hips to help this time.

She got the jeans down to his lower calves before she had to swing one leg to the side so he could finish the job. Giving her plenty of time to study his anatomy—*all* of his anatomy.

He fished a non-latex condom from his pocket before dropping the jeans to the floor.

"Let me." Snatching the package from his grasp, she resumed her seat above him and studied the directions. Folded down the edge of the foil and made a tear in it, pulling until a strip of the square came away.

She hadn't expected it to be so small. Or for her fingers to get sticky when she took it from the package.

Looking at him, then at the prophylactic in her hand, she raised her eyebrows. "Are you sure this thing is going to cover you?"

Roger burst out laughing. Grabbed her around the waist and kissed her until she forgot all about the size of the condom and the size of his erection. At least until it swelled impatiently against her hip.

She pushed at his shoulders until he let her up. "Roll over again."

"Yes, ma'am."

Straddling his prone body once more, she examined the condom in her hand. Stuck her finger in the center and tested the viscosity of the lubrication. Rolled the edges and wondered again how there could possibly be enough material here to sheath the impressive length and girth of him.

She finally handed it to him, not wanting to poke a hole in it. "It's all yours."

He had it on in seconds.

"Well, call me impressed." She fingered the thin material covering him and marveled at the way he jerked beneath her touch. "And flattered again."

"Are you going to play with me all night, darling?"

Meeting his gaze, she recognized the lust there. Tempered by patience. Waiting for her to give him that final signal.

Her nose tickled, and she blinked as tears welled in her eyes. "You are the sweetest man."

"Islanders in Papua New Guinea used sugarcane for sweets in 4000 B.C."

"What? Oh."

He held the hem of her gown in his hand, that fun fact embroidered in a line above the black lace edging.

"Let me see." Pretending to read it, even though she'd sewed it on herself, she pulled the material up her thighs, then flung it off over her head.

"I don't want to vie for your attention," she explained, enjoying his appreciative smile as she leaned over his chest and licked the tendon at the side of his neck.

"I'm all yours."

"Show me."

Those magic hands had her groaning in seconds. Seeking his lips, his touch, his heat, because nothing in her life had ever felt as good as his body intertwined with hers. Until he finally came inside her. Paused while she caught her breath and adjusted to the feeling of him. Glided in and out while she quivered and undulated above him.

She loved being on top. It meant he didn't have to support himself and his hands were free to roam her back, stroke her breasts, guide her movements. She was a woman. Powerful. Sexy. And, most importantly, free.

When her orgasm rushed over her and she lost her

rhythm, he held her fast, then lifted his hips and thrust his way through the spasms, sending tiny aftershocks to every nerve ending in her body until she was a limp pile of limbs sprawled on top of him.

"Did you?" she slurred, replete but not sure if he found his release. Having never done this before, she really couldn't be certain.

"Don't you worry about me, darling." He kissed her ear and pulled the comforter up, tucking it around her shoulders. "Everything was perfect."

****

Sun streamed in through the bedroom windows, letting her know the time was well past her usual five o'clock alarm. The clock face was turned away from her, toward the corner, and Mischief was a purring orange ball on the pillow where Roger's head had been.

Sounds and smells from the kitchen told her he was out there making breakfast. She closed her eyes and said a quick prayer of thanksgiving for Roger, last night, and their relationship.

She should probably get up and help him. Play hostess.

Instead, she stretched beneath the comforter and enjoyed the luxury of a personal day off, lying in bed and letting the soft material caress her naked body. So decadent. Like skinny-dipping all over again. Only better.

"You're almost as boneless as that cat."

His words from the doorway made her yelp with surprise.

"Sorry, didn't mean to scare you."

"Come here and scare me again," she all but purred.

He crossed the carpet and gave her a kiss that lingered yet still had her pouting for more when he stepped back. "Coffee's ready."

"How long have you been awake?"

"A couple hours."

She sat up and searched the rumpled bedding for her nightgown. "You should have woken me." She found the satin slip between folds in the comforter, shook it out, and pulled it on over her head before putting her bare feet on the floor.

"I like watching you sleep."

Oh. She couldn't think of anything to say to that. Such an intimate comment, making her warm and light inside.

"Better get back to the bacon or it'll burn."

Right. "I'll meet you out there."

With a buss on her cheek, he returned to the kitchen while she dashed into the bathroom.

"Ugh. I can't believe he kissed *that*," she said to her reflection in the mirror. Clumps of hair stood at odd angles from her head. Good thing she couldn't see the rest of her face. "Oh, my God." She clapped her hand over her mouth because he'd kissed her before she brushed her teeth! So much worse than her hair sticking out like Medusa.

"Breakfast is ready."

"Coming."

A couple of minutes later, she emerged wearing a fleece robe and pink cheeks. Looking adorable and cuddly, but he felt compelled to say, "I kind of liked the other look," even as he pulled her close for a thorough kiss. "Hmm. Fresh mint flavor."

"I can't believe I kissed you before brushing my

teeth. You couldn't have enjoyed that."

"I like everything about you, darling." He had never been more sincere, but just to make sure his words didn't scare her off, he lightheartedly flicked the zipper tab on her robe. "In fact, even this has possibilities."

Anything that gave him better access to her soft, warm body was okay by him.

"You can play with it later." Her husky words and accompanying smile had him adjusting his jeans before he sat down next to her. "But first, we eat. I'm hungry. Somebody kept me up late last night."

"And what a night it was."

They talked desultorily while eating bacon and eggs.

"I thought poor Emmeline might pass out," he admitted, "being in front of a crowd and everything."

"Fifty people, tops."

"Ten is a crowd to her." He finished his coffee, put another pod in the machine, and took their now-empty plates to the sink. "She and Trevor used to play together when they were little. Maybe the only time she let go of her mother was when he was around."

"One-on-one must be her strength, then. Patients love her."

The coffee finished percolating, and he poured half into her cup, half into his own before rejoining her at the table. "How about a little one-on-one for me?"

He patted his thigh, and she moved from her chair to his lap where they sipped their coffee in silence, her leaning back against him, his arm draped loosely over her hip. He enjoyed the sun coming through the windows, admired the evergreen swags and holly berries adorning the sills.

"Jonnie did a nice job decorating," he remembered. "The function room looked just like a church."

"It did. Of course, if I ever get married, it will be at the church in town."

"What do you mean, of course?" He didn't really have an objection, figured as the bride it was her right to choose the venue—*whoa!* Where had that thought come from?

"Well, my sister would have a fit if I went anywhere else."

Now he really was puzzled. "Why would Hazel care? She doesn't even want you having a relationship."

Lisa turned a puzzled expression on him. "How do you know that?"

Uh-oh. Time to come clean. "Your sister paid me a visit the day after Thanksgiving. You know, after we went to Syracuse together."

"I don't even have to ask you what she said." Her hazel green eyes flashed with fury, and her body stiffened in his hold. "She had no right to do that."

"Don't worry, I made it clear we were grown-ups and perfectly capable of running our lives without any assistance from her."

"Thank you." Relaxing in his hold again, she took a drink of coffee before adding, "She means well. And I do care what she thinks, some of the time, but I already have one mother."

"Hmm." He emptied his mug and put it down on the table. "But you still want her approval?" At her questioning look, he reminded her, "You said she'd have a fit if you didn't get married at the church in town."

"Oh. Right. She's the minister there."

She could have knocked him down with a feather. He sat up and held her a few inches from his chest so he could see her face. "You're serious?"

"I'm sorry. I didn't know how to tell you."

He could see from her tight expression, brow puckered, mouth turned down, how sharing this information upset her.

"It's not exactly a great lead-in for dating, you know?" Her attempt at flippancy couldn't hide her continued apprehension. "Yes, she's the minister. Went into the family business."

"You come from a family of ministers?" An uneasy feeling curled in the pit of his stomach.

"Yeah, that's why she gave me grief for missing church to watch your hockey game. I go every Sunday. And to the Bible study and potluck every Wednesday night."

"I didn't know that."

"Is it a big deal?"

"Not to me. You can believe whatever you want to believe." That had always been his motto, but he wasn't sure it would be that easy for the two of them.

As if to confirm that, she slid off his lap and back onto her chair. "I believe in God." The distance between them was fast becoming a chasm. "I'm a Christian."

"Okay."

"What about you? I assume your family is Christian, too, but Catholic instead of Protestant. Am I right?"

"Some people in my family are."

"And you?"

He took a deep breath. Aware his answer could change everything between them. "I don't believe in God, Lisa. I'm an atheist."

She didn't say anything. Just stared at him for the longest time. Even when she finally blinked, her expression didn't change. Every muscle surrounding his heart tensed in full-on protective mode, because what she said next could pierce right through that organ and leave him with nothing but a gaping wound.

She was that important to him. Only weeks ago, he hadn't known she existed. Now he couldn't imagine life without her.

"Is this because of Mindy?"

Not the question he expected, but at least she was talking to him. "It doesn't have anything to do with her."

"You don't blame God, then? For taking her away from you, I mean. For taking her life at such a young age?"

"Hard to blame someone you don't believe in for something millions of other people go through, too."

She sucked a breath in through her teeth. "How long have you felt this way?"

"Since I was a teenager."

"What happened?"

Roger sighed, uncertain if he could answer the question in a way that wouldn't make things worse but knowing there was no point in prevaricating. "I reached the age of reason."

Her gasp said she was offended.

"Let me explain. Please."

She nodded.

"I started learning about other cultures. Native

190

cultures here in the Americas and people on other continents. It seemed to me that every society had something to explain where they came from, and every one of them had some idea about what happens after death. No proof, just rationalization, but it made them feel better. All the rules in between birth and death? Those things that religions fight wars over and think are so important? That's their way of keeping people obedient, keeping them tied to their belief system."

"So you don't think things like *thou shalt not kill* or *thou shalt not steal* are important?"

"Of course, they are. That's why pretty much every society on the planet has those rules in their religions. But that's about society not breaking down and falling apart. It isn't about creation or death or the fate of your soul."

She said nothing. Just sat there like she was chewing over his words, but he didn't think she was considering them. More likely she was trying to decide what to do about his belief system being so different from her own.

Long minutes passed. Mischief padded out of her craft room and wove his long body in and out of her chair legs, but she didn't seem to notice. The cat finally gave up and leaped into her lap for attention. She blinked. Once. Focus returned to her pretty hazel eyes, but when she met his gaze, what he hoped to find wasn't there.

"I'm going to need some time." Her eyes were cloudy, her tone dull. "To think about this."

Me, too. He didn't say the words aloud.

"What are your plans for the day?"

I planned to spend it with you. Apparently that

option was no longer on the table. So he shrugged, made up a few things he needed to do around the farm even though there was no urgency to any of them, then asked what was on her agenda.

"Well, I took the day off. To sleep in after the wedding." Spoken like she wanted him to understand he shouldn't get any other ideas. "I've got a craft fair over in Lancaster on Saturday. I should probably spend a few hours finishing pieces for it. And of course, I still have to do my exercises."

"Of course." Even to his own ears, his voice sounded hollow. Clearing his throat, he tried again. "Would you like me to do the dishes before I go?"

She glanced at the kitchen counter, the sink. "No. You cooked. I'll clean."

An awkward silence fell between them. Like a vacuum without sound or color. Empty. Emotionless or full of emotion, the result was the same, a big black hole.

He scraped his chair back and rose to his feet. "I guess I'll be on my way, then."

"Yes." She stood, one hand gripping the back of her chair.

When he leaned down to give her a kiss, she offered her cheek.

Well, that certainly put him in his place. He crossed the room to the deacon's bench by the door, stuffed his feet into his boots, and grabbed his coat from the peg on the wall. Not until he had his gloves and hat on did he look back at her. She hadn't moved from the table.

"Can I phone you?"

"Sure."

Chapter Sixteen

What an idiot. As soon as his truck left the yard, she wanted to call him back. He had been honest with her from the start, had never pretended to be anything he wasn't, yet she'd sent him away. Only what would she say to him?

Conversion for either one of them was out of the question. Her beliefs were absolute, her early perception of him an accurate one. The man was solid. Steady. Dependable. He also knew his own mind, and she knew enough about him to recognize his beliefs about life and the afterlife were the result of deep introspection and long consideration.

Her own conclusions came from a similar place. She hadn't *inherited* her religion. People often claimed they were raised in the church or brought up in their faith, but that didn't mean they were religious or faithful. As a minister's child, maybe even because she was a minister's child, she'd had to find her belief system for herself. Test it against all other theories and evidence. Accept it not because someone or some book told her to but because she couldn't conceive of anything else being truer than what she arrived at.

So where did that leave them?

Before these thoughts made her crazy, she let go of the chair and washed the few breakfast dishes. Tried not to think about his hands on these items, preparing a meal for her so she could sleep in. Tried not to remember her excitement on waking, knowing he was in the house, anticipating how they might spend their day together.

When that chore was done, she put on her yoga outfit and went through forty-five minutes of poses. She ached in places she didn't normally ache, was more limber in others.

Last night couldn't have been better if she'd written a script for it.

Alone in her shower, she marveled at how sensitive her breasts were, how soaping her belly and thighs evoked memories of his touch. Her eyes slid closed, and she lay her forehead on the tiled walls.

He was the perfect man. Everything she'd learned about him led to that conviction, so she should have been expecting it to blow up in her face this spectacularly.

And she only had herself to blame. She should have introduced Hazel that day as not only her sister but the local minister. Instead, she'd kept that to herself because people were so often scared off when she did. She would never deny her faith, but hadn't she been doing exactly that? Or was it just the speed with which her feelings had developed that kept her from having that conversation?

Dizzy from doubt and self-recrimination, she toddled into the bedroom while toweling her hair dry. Time to make good on her voiced plans for the day. Get dressed. Work on her jewelry stock. Maybe treat herself to a turkey club sandwich from The Common Store.

Roger called her cellphone while she was tying her shoes. She let it go to voicemail.

Mischief complained about his empty food dish. She refilled the dispenser and topped off his water bubbler.

The *Somerset Reporter* arrived. She retrieved the weekly edition from the sleeve by her front door and scanned it for exciting news. Obituaries. Classified ads. Letters to the editor. She tossed it on the table to read the main articles later, then finally ventured into her craft room.

And came to an abrupt halt.

Propped up on her worktable was a large piece of paper from her sketchpad with two drawings. One of herself in her caped jumpsuit, dancing in the arms of a man who had his back to the artist. A man with square-tipped fingers, a lean muscular frame, and a tiny bald spot on the back of his dark head. In the picture she was smiling, all her attention centered on him, the other dancers vague outlines in the background.

The second sketch portrayed her asleep in bed with Mischief curled up on the pillow beside her. Morning light coming through the window kissed her bare shoulders and highlighted the serene expression on her face.

At the bottom of the drawing, he'd signed his name, *R. D. Plankey*. It was the title at the top that did her in, though. *My Gal.*

She fell into her chair and finally gave in to tears.

****

Across town, Roger was sitting at the kitchen table wondering what to do with his day. Glen was gone by the time he got home, so he hadn't been forced to answer any questions about his night, something his brother had a right to ask about since he'd covered morning chores for him just so he could have that night.

Unfortunately, Wednesday was his mother's housecleaning day. When she came into the room with the broom in her hand and a carefully veiled look of inquiry on her face, he stood and made excuses for leaving.

He did errands in town. Returned home and did his laundry, working on some equipment maintenance in the barns while it washed, visiting with and grooming Bets while it dried. He stopped to have a late lunch only when he saw his mother's car leave the yard.

Wednesday was also library day. Something they used to do together because he loved to read as much as she did, but recently she and a group of women had been meeting up for book discussion, so he went later in the afternoon. Alone.

That gave him at least another hour's reprieve. He could think about Lisa and why she hadn't answered his call when he knew she was home and whether or not she would ever take his call again.

They hadn't been apart more than a few hours, and already he missed her. Her smile. Her humor. The way she dove into things completely outside her wheelhouse, saying, "Not a clue," when asked if she knew what she was doing.

How had something so perfect gone so wrong in the blink of an eye?

The knock on the front door was a surprise. Even more startling was who he found standing on the porch.

"You said Malachi could play with your dog," Jonnie reminded him after they exchanged greetings. "Is this a good time?"

"Couldn't be better." A distraction from his

thoughts, even if it came in the form of Lisa's best friend. Judging from her open expression, she didn't know what had happened between them this morning.

"I should probably introduce them," he said on realizing seconds had passed without words between them, but before he could say more, Sadie came barreling around the corner of the house and leaped up onto the porch. Malachi squealed with delight and took off running.

"Looks like love at first sight to me."

"I'll say."

The little boy was rolling around in the snow while Sadie alternately barked circles around him and moved in to slobber canine kisses on his happy face.

"How long have you got?"

"Half an hour?" She posed the reply as a question. "That's when Elijah gets out of school."

Perfect. Calling Sadie to heel, he stepped down from the porch and helped Malachi to his feet. "Why don't I show you and your mom around the yards? That way when you come next time, you'll already know Sadie's favorite spots to play."

"Okay." Bright dark eyes shone with joy above Sadie's silky brown head. "I wore my new boots so we can walk in the snow."

"That's what I like. A young man who thinks ahead."

Half an hour later Sadie was ready to jump into the SUV and go home with them. Roger held her back, listening to her whine while Jonnie buckled her son into his car seat.

"Thank you so much for this."

He inclined his head and fist-bumped Malachi

before she closed the car door.

"Would Friday be a good day for us to come again? Same time?"

"You bet."

When they pulled out of the yard, he turned back to the house because in half an hour the evening milking began, and if he was going to talk to his mother, he might as well get it over with. She had returned home while he was showing his guests around the farm. Now he found her in the kitchen filling the woodstove. Her beautiful silver-streaked hair was coiled in a loose bun at the back of her head, her high cheekbones glowing in the light of the flame. She was an attractive and strong woman, even in her sixties, and he knew if he laid everything on her slim shoulders, she would stand up straight and bear the burden for him.

But he was forty-five years old and had learned to keep his own counsel a long time ago.

She closed the woodstove door and hung the poker on a metal hook above the hearth. "I was hoping we'd have a few minutes alone before chores."

"Oh?" Pretending he didn't know what she wanted to talk about.

She tilted her head and gave him a quizzical look but didn't call him out on his evasive reply. It had always been this way between them. She'd treated him like a man, even when he was a child, and she let him decide when and how, or even if, to share his troubles.

"Zeb and Carolyn found a place in South Carolina. They're going to fly down there to sign on it after Christmas."

"That was quick." They had only started looking a few weeks ago.

"Hmm. They hope to move up their retirement date, maybe as early as this spring, since Bryce will be done with school in May."

"Oh." His son and nephew could work the summer, but Colin still had three years of college left. They'd have to hire at least one more hand to get through until then.

"Your father and I will probably be out of here by June. You can do any remodeling you need to then." When he didn't say anything, she added, "Maybe install a walk-in shower in our bathroom?"

For the first time in years, his throat hurt from holding back emotion. He blinked, shook his head once, and looked away from those beautiful, perceptive blue eyes. Right now his feelings were too raw to process or share.

Laying her warm palm against his cheek, she said, "*Ça va marcher, fils.*"

****

Things will work out, he reminded himself while he went about his chores the next day. Up at four. Milk the cows. Rinse the alleys. Feed. Water. Meet the milk truck. Sterilize the holding tanks. Go through mail and email. Replace flashing on the roof above the door to the small barn.

Through it all he waited for her call. Checked the phone in the entryway because that one was connected to the answering machine, but no light blinked red to indicate a message. Nothing written on the magnetic shopping list on the refrigerator next to the phone extension in the kitchen. While the farm was a home, it was also a business, and everyone knew to record messages.

With still no call after evening chores and supper, he drove to her house. They were both adults. As far as he was concerned, the only thing they couldn't do was avoid one another. Best to have a conversation about this distance between them and figure out how it could be bridged.

The lights were on when he arrived, two cars parked in the driveway below the carport. He angled his truck to the side in case they needed to leave before he did and went right up to the front door as if he were expected.

Darcy answered his knock. "Hey, Uncle Roger! Good thing you're here, because we made gingerbread cookies, and the boys need a judge to decide which ones taste best. We used two recipes and split up into Team Darcy and Team Chelsea. Lisa says she can't pick a winner because she helped us all. Hey, Preston! Hey, Elijah! Our favorite judge is here."

****

Lisa was bombarded with emotions at the sight of him standing inside her door. Longing. Excitement. Sadness. Confusion. She wanted to rush over and throw her arms around him, inhale his clean outdoor scent, and forget everything that had happened yesterday morning.

Instead, she stood where she was beside the kitchen island, trying not to devour him with her gaze. Trying to act natural in front of the girls and their little helpers.

Preston came to her rescue. "Hey, Slick, we made a huuuge batch of cookies! We have to let them cool now, but on Sunday we can frost them all and put strings in them to hang on our Christmas trees."

"Malachi is gonna help decorate them," Elijah

added.

"So you have to taste both and let them know what you think," Darcy urged. "But it should be a blind taste test, right? Lisa, do you have anything we can use for a blindfold?"

Startled out of her preoccupation with his dark hair, strong jaw, and the lines of fatigue around his eyes—had he lost as much sleep as she had last night?—she nodded. Words were beyond her right now.

In her craft room she took a length of silk from a drawer, then returned to find Roger seated at the table with his coat off, waiting for the taste test.

Her stomach fell as she approached him. Neither one of them spoke. She rolled the silk with hands that trembled, hoping no one would notice, and slipped the fabric over his eyes, tying the ends just below the tiny bald spot she loved so much. "Is that too tight?"

Her question was a whisper of sound.

"It's fine," he said in a voice as low as her spirits.

"Perfect!" Darcy exclaimed, grabbing his hands and placing a cookie in each one. "Now take a bite from the left, then the right, and tell us which tastes the best."

"I'm gonna need some milk, pumpkin. Can't eat gingerbread cookies without milk."

"Oh!" Darcy slapped herself on the forehead. "Lisa, is it okay if he has a cup of milk?"

"Of course."

"I'll get it," Chelsea volunteered. "A dairy farmer has to have milk with his dessert, right, Mr. Plankey?" She put the glass down on the table, but he couldn't take it with his hands still holding two cookies.

"I thought I told you to call me Roger."

"Oh, sorry."

The girl blushed, and Lisa envied her innocence. Not so long ago he could cause the same reaction from her with just a few words.

"Roger, the milk is straight in front of you, but if you need help, I can hand it to you after the first bite."

He tasted one cookie and washed it down. Tasted the second and did the same. Proclaimed them a dead tie, much to the disappointment of the little boys and the delight of the girls. Lisa had expected no less. She'd known he wouldn't choose a winner.

"Well, we've got to get these two home for bedtime. Preston, you're riding with me. Chelsea's going to run Elijah up to The Gables."

Roger removed the scarf and handed it to Lisa. She folded it into smaller and smaller squares while trying to think of something to say.

How to break the ice? And if she did, what then?

Belatedly, she put the scarf down and helped dress the boys in their outerwear.

Long moments after waving the foursome off at the door, she stood facing that portal.

"Are you going to stare at it all night?"

A quiver ran through her at the sound of his voice. Familiar. Precious.

His chair scraped across the floor. Footsteps approached. Warmth surrounded her even though he didn't touch her, and every inhale brought his scent into her lungs.

"I don't know where we go from here," she finally admitted on a strangled whisper.

"Facing me would be a start."

So rational. So mature. While she had never felt more out of control and uncertain in her life.

His hand on her shoulder, rather than adding to her turmoil, grounded her and gave her strength to turn around. But when it came to meeting his gaze, a brief glimpse was all she could manage.

"Can't even look me in the eye, Lisa?"

He rarely used her name. It was always gal or darling. If he used the last, she'd probably dissolve into a hot mess, yet she wanted desperately to hear that endearment from him. Wanted so much to let him take the lead, solve the problem, and take the responsibility from her.

"I need more time to figure this out."

"Okay." He buttoned his coat and drew on his gloves. "You'll call me?"

"Sure."

Chapter Seventeen

Of course, she didn't call him. Friday came and went under heavy skies laden with the weight of an impending storm. When he finished milking Saturday morning and came out of the barn to four inches of snow and more falling at a steady rate, he slapped some cheese between two pieces of bread and ate them on his way into town.

Lisa was outside her house, filling the trunk of her car with boxes of jewelry.

"Tell me you're not making this trip today." Days of frustration came out in the demand.

"Hello to you, too," was her flip greeting, followed by, "What does it look like?"

"It looks like you're being foolish. Did you even watch the weather forecast?"

Another car pulled into the yard. Hazel.

"I came to give you a ride to Lancaster. That is if you're still bent on making this trip even though you shouldn't."

"Did you two plan this?" Lisa snapped.

"You told her the same thing?" Hazel asked with surprise.

"Yes, but she's not listening." Lifting a plastic tub from the pile beside her car, he said, "If you're determined to do this, at least let me drive you."

Lisa wrenched the tub from his grasp and put it in

her trunk. "I can handle it."

He removed the tub and closed the trunk lid, leaning against it with his hip to keep her from opening it again. "Don't be stubborn."

"She's the queen of stubborn."

"I am right here!" Shoving him, she popped the trunk lid with her key, and rather than hurt her, he moved out of the way. "I've got a craft fair to attend. You can both leave."

"I'll go." Hazel stepped back. "It looks like you're in good hands, anyway. Call me when you get there."

Lisa ignored her.

Roger waited until they were alone again before putting his hand on the last tub as Lisa reached for it. "We're expecting ten to fourteen inches. Not light stuff, either."

"It's not my first time driving in snow."

"But it's a long drive. If you break down, what will you do?"

"Call 9-1-1."

"Can you at least look at me when I'm talking to you! Dammit, Lisa, I'm trying to make sure you're safe, and you're acting like I'm the one being unreasonable!"

She did look up then, hazel eyes spitting fire. "I didn't ask for your help. And I don't need it. Would you be this way if I didn't have spina bifida?"

He took a step back as if she'd punched him. "That's what you think this is about? I have never, ever treated you like an invalid."

She put the last tub in her car and closed the lid. Opened the driver's side door but, before getting in, looked back at him with eyes devoid of any spark and said, "You just did."

He was still standing there slack-jawed when her taillights disappeared at the end of the drive. A few hundred yards away but already swallowed up by the storm.

"Well, hell."

He didn't know how concern for her well-being had turned into such a spectacular disaster, but nothing had changed. She was still making a sixty-mile trip in heavy snow on roads she didn't normally travel. He hopped in the truck and reversed out of her yard.

Seeing no sign of her up on the common, he pulled into The Common Store and asked Chelsea if he could borrow a phone. He really wished phone booths were still a thing, because the deli was loud and busy, but at the same time Chelsea had his niece's number stored in her contacts, and he had a better chance of reaching her on her own cell than through his brother's landline.

"Hey, girlfriend, did Bryce deliver last night?"

"I did not just hear that."

"Uncle Roger!" Darcy wailed while Chelsea's face turned as red as the raspberries she was adding to a blender.

Under normal circumstances, he would play this out, but he had more important things on his mind and limited time to banter. "I need to know where the lady with the Bible verses lives."

"What?"

"You said there's a lady who gives out religious stuff on Halloween. Is she in her thirties with brown hair?"

"Yeah."

"That's Pastor Hazel," Chelsea volunteered, "but she also gives out candy."

"Do you know where she lives?"

She nodded, fitting the top to the blender and turning it on.

"Never mind, pumpkin. Talk to you later."

He disconnected the call and passed the phone over the counter to his son's girlfriend.

"Her house is at the bottom of Pleasant Street. Olive-green cape with white trim and a red door."

Finding it was easy, waiting for Hazel to answer his knock interminable. Around him the snow fell so hard he had to blink to keep it from accumulating on his eyelashes. How far had Lisa got to already? Was he going to find her in a ditch somewhere or worse?

The door opened. "I thought you were going with my sister?"

"She took off without me. Where is this craft fair? I'm going to follow her."

She ushered him inside while she looked up the address of the elementary school in Lancaster. "It's normally at the Episcopal Church, but they were having some problem with the heat, so they moved it." She tore a piece of notepaper from a pad on the secretary near the door and wrote the address down for him. "That's my phone number at the bottom if you need it."

"Do you know what route she's taking?"

Hazel sighed. "Yes. She's taking 114, then going west on 105. I tried to get her to at least go to St. Johnsbury and pick up 93 to Littleton, but she said interstates are the worst roads to be on in a storm."

"She's right about that. No visibility." He read the paper, took out his wallet, and put it inside. "Maybe I can catch up with her."

"She won't thank you for it."

He shrugged. Her annoyance measured against her safety? No contest.

"But I will. She's lucky to have someone else who cares about her."

"I'd better make tracks." He pulled the door open to leave, but she added one final caution.

"She won't have any cellphone service by the time she reaches Seymour Lake and probably none through Island Pond. If she goes off the road there, she can't call for help."

"I'll keep my eyes peeled."

****

Lisa's eyes stung from the blast of hot air coming out of the defroster vents in the dash. Her shoulders were tight from leaning over the steering wheel to peer through the heavy snow at the road in front of her. The windshield wipers flipping across her line of vision at maniacal speed were the only thing fast about this trip.

She couldn't go over twenty-five miles per hour. Every time the accelerator needle approached thirty, the car fishtailed. Her fingers hurt from gripping the steering wheel. Her blouse clung to her skin, and her armpits were uncomfortably damp from a combination of full heat setting and nerves, but no way could she stop and remove her jacket. All she could do was plough on through the narrow tunnel created by her headlights and take her half out of the center of the road because she had few tracks to follow.

Stupid, stupid, stupid. She should have listened to Hazel and Roger. Instead, she had overreacted to what now seemed like reasonable concern, and here she was, a sweating, trembling mess on a road without other travelers on her way to a fair where she might come home with a few hundred dollars if she was lucky.

The Sherman tank on her left was barely visible, but she blew out a breath on seeing its dark outline because that meant she was approaching the intersection at Island Pond. Halfway between Montreal and Portland, Maine, if she was traveling on the old Grand Trunk Railway.

If only that service still ran.

She didn't know how many miles she'd covered by car, because her navigation system and cellphone reminded her there was no service here, but at least she'd reached civilization. She could pull into the parking lot of the Kingdom Market grocery store. Sit and wait for the worst of the storm to pass. Or do the smart thing—turn around and go home, admitting her pride had overridden her common sense.

Instead, she crawled past the line of little homes crowding the road, made a slow wide arc through the open intersection, and continued on her journey. Away from homes and businesses. Through lonely forest made dark by the storm despite it being early morning. She had a mug of coffee in the cupholder between the front seats but didn't touch it. The radio played nothing but static, adding to the surreal and spooky atmosphere, but she didn't dare move her hands from the wheel to adjust the settings. Just counted herself lucky each time she passed another telephone pole because they confirmed she was still on the road.

She didn't know this part of the state well. When the terrain to her right flattened out, she nervously steered the car a little more to the left in case there was a river. Sometime later she saw abandoned railcars with graffiti painted on the side and realized the tracks ran alongside the road, but the knowledge brought no comfort.

Why hadn't she listened to them?

"Because you're an idiot," she said aloud, immediately regretting it when her windshield fogged up from the heat of her breath meeting cold plexiglass.

A pickup truck went by at double the speed she was traveling. A pair of headlights in the rearview mirror momentarily distracted her from the road. Being reminded that she wasn't the only driver out here should have reassured her, but it meant she didn't have both lanes to herself. When the vehicle behind her closed in, then overtook her car, she cautiously adjusted her position in the lane based on their taillights, but a few minutes later they were gone, and she was back to using telephone poles as guides.

"Please, God, I promise not to be an idiot again if you just get me there safely," she whispered though this probably wouldn't be the last time pride got the best of her practical nature.

By the time she reached the Connecticut River, she was pretty sure she would make it to Lancaster in one piece though maybe not on time. It was supposed to be about a seventy-five-minute drive from Somerset to the elementary school. She checked the dashboard clock only to realize it had taken that long to reach the border, and she had another twenty-plus miles to go.

The loneliest miles she'd ever traveled. New Hampshire evergreens replaced the mixed forest of northern Vermont. Tall, narrow sentinels bearing witness to the isolation of the road she traveled. Once in a while she saw lights in a window, but long stretches of land passed between them. She met few vehicles, and those she did see were all trucks or SUVs. She was able to drive a little faster here, but the road twisted and turned, requiring all her attention. When she came to the sign for Riverside Speedway, she realized a pair of headlights in her rearview mirror had been there for a while.

That gave her some comfort. If she did spin out and go off the road, at least someone would know right away. She wouldn't have to walk through half a foot of fresh snow on feet that couldn't tell her they were frostbitten and possibly lose the rest of her toes. Earlier, more gruesome visions of freezing upside down in her car, suspended from her seat belt, were finally put to rest.

Buildings emerged from the snow. A funeral home. A dollar store. Giving the impression that she was close to her destination, only to disappear behind her as she traveled another long stretch of road with very little on either side of the narrow white track.

By the time the Lancaster fairgrounds came into view, her fingers ached from gripping the steering wheel. The knot between her shoulder blades had a death grip on the muscles of her upper back.

The traffic circle in downtown Lancaster was greasy. People were out and about. Regular Saturday morning activity, forcing her to pay attention to a dozen things going on around her instead of just the tunnel created by her headlights. After the solitude of the long drive, it was almost too much. She was torn between collapsing with relief and crying over this new stress.

When she finally parked her car in the elementary school parking lot, she did both. Slumped over the steering wheel, only to cry out from the pain in her upper back.

"Proof of life," she said to the windshield wipers still flicking back and forth in front of her. Then, bracing herself, she inhaled a deep breath and exhaled slowly while taking inventory of her aches and pains. Her shoulders would recover though it might take a while. Her lower back was mostly numb. Getting out of the car and trudging through the snow would be difficult, even with her crutches. Then she had tubs of jewelry to carry and a table to set up.

A glance at her cellphone showed ten minutes before the winter market and craft fair opened. No way could she have everything done in that short space of time.

"You do what you can," her mother always said. Which reminded her she still had to let Hazel know she had arrived safely. Calling her sister's number, she slid her seat back and stretched her legs while waiting for her to pick up.

"Lisa?"

"The one and only." Even to her own ears, she sounded tired. Stretching her spine to wake herself up, she said, "I just got here."

"I was worried."

Duh. Jonnie had been right when she said it was a permanent condition. At the same time, she had to admit, "It wasn't a good drive. If the weather hasn't improved by the time the fair ends, I'll rent a room here and come home in the morning."

"Oh."

"I'll call you and let you know, okay? I've got to go now to set up my table."

"Okay. Good luck with the fair."

She turned to put her phone in her purse and shrieked when someone rapped on the car window behind her. Hand to chest, struggling to breathe, she looked through the fogged-up plexiglass. A takeout coffee cup in a gloved hand filled her line of vision. Rolling down her window, she took the pink-and-orange-lettered cup and said, "Someone certainly knows how to get my attention."

"Oh, good. You're speaking to me again."

Lisa paused with the cup halfway to her lips. This was an even bigger surprise than the aroma tempting her taste buds. "I thought I left you in Somerset."

"I've been behind you since a little after Island Pond." He bent and put his forearm on the open windowsill, handsome face in the gap above it. Gaze solemn, he asked, "Are you okay, darling?"

She swallowed the hard lump in her throat and cursed the moisture gathering in her eyes. Unable to speak, afraid to blink, she simply nodded.

"Looks like you made it just in time." They watched some brave soul struggling to wheel a cart of plastic tubs through what must have been almost a foot of snow. "Can I help you set up your jewelry table?"

"Yes." Nothing had changed between them, but she would be a fool to turn down his offer, and she had already met her quota for foolish behavior today. "Thank you."

Chapter Eighteen

Three hours later she was thanking him again, this time for watching her table during a restroom break, though he had proved himself invaluable half a dozen times between setup and breakdown.

The table was long and had the fold-out, snap-in-place kind of legs. She would have had to prop it against something to keep it from closing or falling over while working on one end before she could get to the other. He was tall enough and strong enough that he could hold it with one hand while pulling the legs out. Lucky man.

She'd brought small bills with her for making change but ran out of ones in the first hour. He went to the bank down the street and got more.

When the number of shoppers dwindled about thirty minutes before closing time, he began making trips to her car with tubs of inventory, so by the time the doors closed, she had only those items on display to pack and carry out.

He wouldn't let her do that, of course.

"There's a lot of snow on the ground," he explained when she started to argue, "and it's not the powdery kind. I saw two people wipe out crossing the parking lot, and they weren't dealing with crutches, too."

"I'd have to do it myself if you weren't here."

"Well, now you don't have to."

So she followed him out of the school and almost lost her footing within a yard of the main entrance. A nightmare for anyone with crutches, because instinct meant holding on to them instead of bracing for a fall. After that, she made sure to synchronize her foot and crutch movements and reached the car without mishap.

Roger had started the engine on his last trip outside. He had scraped the windows and brushed off the roof, too, but already those surfaces were coated with a fresh layer of snow, and her windshield wipers were crusted with a quarter inch of thick, wet sludge.

He put the last of her things in the trunk and slammed the lid closed. "Do you want to get lunch somewhere?"

She was hungry, but the snow showed no signs of letting up. "I should probably head back, don't you think? While it's still light out?"

"There's a sandwich shop down the street. We could be eating in five minutes, on the road in twenty."

It took thirty. After the meal, they filled their gas tanks, and she called Hazel to let her know she was leaving before beginning the long trek home to Somerset.

His headlights in the rearview mirror gave her more comfort than she was ready to admit.

At her house he helped unload her plastic tubs. She gave him a gingerbread cookie for his trouble, and he gave her a kiss on the cheek.

Awkward. She would have delved into her feelings, tried to figure out where she was at and where to go from here, but as soon as she sat down in the living room, she fell sound asleep.

215

Hours later she woke to Mischief complaining about an empty food dish. A glance at the clock showed it was after seven. She filled his dispenser, stroked his back a few times, and started the tub. While the warm water mixed with a few drops of floral scent, she called Jonnie.

"Hey," her friend greeted in a groggy voice.

"Am I interrupting a nap?"

"Not yet, but pregnancy is kicking my butt right now. I can't seem to keep my eyes open much past five o'clock."

"Oh, I'm sorry. You want me to call back tomorrow?"

"No, I'm good. What's up?"

Now that she had her friend on the line, she wasn't sure where to begin. She had intentionally kept Wednesday morning's discovery to herself, needing time to process it, but she was no less confused now than she had been then.

"Hey? You okay?"

"I'm not sure."

"Well, I have a good friend who likes to say, 'Just spit it out.' Sound advice, by the way."

Lisa smiled at Jonnie turning her own expression on her. "Okay. Remember when I said I was scared because Roger is perfect?"

Half an hour later she lay in the tub, relaxed but resolute. Jonnie was right. Some secrets destroyed lives, and she was upset now because she hadn't told Roger who she was. Upset because she missed him but didn't know how to share her life with him. Afraid to disappoint her family or, worse, lose them. Instead of giving her loved ones a chance, she was shutting them all out. Including Roger. Especially him.

****

Church was sparsely attended the next day, ironic since Christmas was fast approaching, but she still couldn't get her sister alone for a full half hour following the service. When the doors finally closed on the last member of the congregation, she took a deep breath and said, "I need to talk to you."

"Okay." Hazel was at the lectern putting her sermon in her briefcase and didn't look up.

"Haze."

She probably hadn't called her by that nickname in years, and not surprisingly, it got her attention.

"What's wrong?"

"Nothing's wrong. I mean, it could be, but that depends on how you take this."

Hazel put her briefcase on the floor beside the pulpit, then stepped down off the dais to sit in the first pew. She didn't pat the space beside her, but she might as well have. Lisa released her crutches, rested them against the end of the pew, and joined her.

Before she lost her nerve, she took a deep breath and dove in. "Roger is an atheist."

The roof remained intact.

"I didn't know it when I met him, and he didn't know I was a Christian."

"Because you didn't tell him."

Was that accusation or supposition?

"You like people to get to know you first before you tell them."

Lisa shrugged her shoulders. *Truth.* She hadn't revealed her faith to Jonnie until she was certain they would be friends regardless of any difference in beliefs.

"The curse of being a minister's child—" Hazel sighed. "—and living in the least-religious state in the nation."

"Unless the Gallup polls have changed." Any other time they might have laughed at that fact. They reviewed those numbers annually while their parents lamented at losing them both to this "godforsaken part of the country."

"When did you find out?"

"Last Wednesday."

"That's why you didn't want his help yesterday."

Definitely supposition this time.

"You can talk to me, Lisa." At her one-shouldered shrug, Hazel continued, "I know you think I'm a pain and that I worry too much, but not everything I say is a judgment. And you can't live your life worrying about whether or not I will approve."

"I don't."

"You pretend not to." Her sister smiled, eyes the same shade as her own warm with understanding. "But tell me, what do you plan to do about this? He seems like a great guy, and he certainly cares about you. I went to see him, you know."

"He told me."

"You should have heard him fighting your corner. I only wish I had a man who would stand up for me like that."

"You? Want a man?" Lisa teased, but the smile fell from her lips as soon as she saw her sister's reaction. Real pain clouded her eyes. "Oh, my God, Hazel, what happened to you?"

Now it was her sister's turn to shrug. "Remember when I worked as an auditor after college? To get my

CPA license before I started seminary?"

Lisa nodded. Her smart little sister had known, even then, that she would need one occupation to support the other.

"We met then. He was on leave from the army. Stationed in Afghanistan."

Brown head bent, she ran her plain, neatly manicured fingernail along the seam of a red hymnal, then put it beneath a Bible and straightened both books on the pew. "I lost him," she whispered. "Sniper's bullet, they told me." When she lifted her gaze, moisture pooled at the edge of her eyelashes, but no tears fell. "He didn't even get the chance to defend himself."

"It was serious?"

"I introduced him to Mom and Dad."

"How is it I never heard about this before?"

"They didn't approve of our relationship." She reached over and twined her fingers with Lisa's own like they had done as little girls. "He was Jewish." At her intake of breath, Hazel continued. "I regret every day that I didn't defend him and our relationship. Instead, I sent him away not knowing if I'd be waiting for him when he got home. Now I'll wait for him forever."

"You'll meet someone," Lisa said lamely. "Someday."

Hazel shook her head. "I don't think so." With a squeeze of her fingers, she let Lisa's hand drop. "But I'm not going to let you make the same mistake I did. If I'm right, you love this man."

"I do." She hadn't admitted it before, and saying it aloud almost made her dizzy.

"Then let me help you tell them. You'll be calling them tonight?"

"Yes." Their usual Sunday night video call.

"I'll come over. Seven o'clock?"

"Sounds good. Thanks, Haze."

Her sister nodded. She picked up her briefcase, and Lisa grabbed her crutches. In the vestibule they donned their outerwear, then walked together down the neatly shoveled brick path to the parking lot behind the church. Their cars looked lonely amid almost two feet of fresh snow.

"I'll see you later," Hazel said, waiting as she always did for Lisa to get in her car and be safely on her way before getting into her own.

Driving up onto the common and around to Pleasant Street, Lisa realized she felt lighter than she had in days. Who knew a talk with her sister could lift such a burden from her heart?

****

Roger was surprised to hear from her on Monday. "The girls and I are making coconut curry chicken tomorrow after work," she said when he answered the phone. "Would you like to come for supper?"

"Of course."

He didn't know if it would be just the two of them or the four of them, but he made a run to Newport midday so he could get something for her and still be back in time to play with Sadie and Malachi before evening chores. Because the snow was so deep, he took the little boy and his mother through the calf barn and introduced them to Bets, who wanted nothing to do with them. Sadie more than made up for her lack of welcome, following Malachi up and down the alley like a lovelorn teenager while he chatted away to her about everything and nothing.

"This is so good for him," Jonnie said. "I can't thank you enough."

"No thanks necessary. I'd much rather have him hanging around than the reality-show people."

"Amen to that. It's good money, but we definitely worked for every penny. I think David might have convinced them to look into another location for next year." She patted her rounded tummy. "We'll have enough on our hands with the regular business and our family."

"Have you come up with a name yet?"

"David is certain it's a girl, even though we're not having a test to find out, and he's still talking about Jonquil. I told him I'd file for divorce if he used that name."

Roger grinned because even after knowing her only a short time, he could tell that was an empty threat. "Jonquils are the ones that come up in the spring, right? When there's still snow on the ground?"

"That's them. Terrible name. I don't know how my mother ever chose it, but no way are we making it a tradition. Might just as well call her Carnation."

The arrangement he bought for Lisa in Newport had carnations in it. He wasn't sure if she had any preferences, only that she liked flowers, and since her house was decorated in red and green for Christmas with white candles in the windows, he told the florist to put something together that would complement those colors. When Lisa opened the door to let him in, he handed her a bouquet of white carnations, miniature red roses, holly berries, and greens. "You said you sometimes splurge on flowers," he reminded her when she accepted them, telling him he didn't have to, "so I thought you'd like these."

"Oh, so romantic, Uncle Roger."

"Hey, pumpkin. I keep forgetting to ask you. How'd your Montreal trip go?"

"Awesome. I got a beautiful music box for Mémère for Christmas, but don't tell her."

"My lips are sealed."

He removed his coat, and Lisa took the flowers to the kitchen sink.

"Hi, Chelsea."

"Hey, Mr.—I mean, Roger."

"Seeing my boy at the end of the week?"

Her blush was instant and bright.

"Don't tease," Lisa chided. "She and Darcy worked hard tonight. Hope you're hungry?"

"Always."

"Good." She unwrapped the flowers and snipped the ends off the stems. "Go ahead and have a seat. I'll be right with you."

He pulled out a chair and sat between the two girls, hanging his hat on the seat back and pouring himself a glass of milk from the jug on the table. Darcy passed him a roll, and he buttered it before giving the knife and butter dish to Chelsea.

When Lisa leaned past him to put the vase in the center of the table, she kissed the bald spot on the back of his head. "These are perfect for the holidays. Thank you."

He wasn't foolish enough to think this meant everything was okay, but it was something, and right now he would take anything she had to offer. Before meeting her, he hadn't known anything was missing from his life. Since last Wednesday, it had been as empty as a crypt.

"Hope you like cayenne pepper, Mr.—Roger."

Half an hour later the girls were gone, but the heat of the meal lingered on his tongue. Lisa commented on it when he reached for the milk jug to refill his glass.

"Curry got to you?"

"It's just spicier than my usual diet."

"I have some wine."

"Oh?"

"I bought it last week. In case you… Well, never mind. Would you like a glass now?"

"Sure."

He watched as she opened a lower kitchen cabinet and pulled out a bottle. Not just any bottle, either, but Burning Desire from the Hard Row to Hoe winery, a vintage she would know he liked. The fact that she remembered had to be a good sign.

"I hope you don't mind regular glasses?"

"That's fine." He would drink it from her hand if it was all she had. Anything to spend more time with her.

She placed a water goblet in front of him and poured a couple of inches of red wine into it, then served herself and joined him at the table. "It hasn't had time to breathe."

He didn't want to make small talk, yet it seemed to be all she was capable of. Eventually, even that petered out until they were sitting only feet from one another staring at the glasses in their hands.

Time to scale the mountain between them.

"Tell me something, Lisa. Why do you believe in God?"

He'd meant it when he said she had a right to her beliefs, and he didn't have any problem with people having different beliefs than his own, but he wondered if hers came from her parents schooling her in their faith or if she had arrived at them through her own inquiry and self-reflection.

The silence stretched on for so long he had almost given up on getting an answer when she said, "I told you about losing my toe."

She played with the glass in her hand, and he sensed she was somewhere else right now.

"I didn't tell you that I almost died during surgery. Not because of the bone infection, but because of the latex allergy. We didn't know about it yet because it takes more than one exposure to provoke a reaction."

Uncertain if she would welcome his touch just then, he nevertheless reached over and put his hand over hers. Her fingers stilled, but she didn't remove them.

"I went into anaphylactic shock. Died for a moment on the table."

His heart seized up at the thought. He could have lost her before he even knew she existed. Might never have seen her pretty smile, her apple cheeks, and meadow-green eyes.

"Anyway, I remember every minute of it. I can tell you, word for word, what everyone in the room was saying while I was out. And I can tell you what I saw."

"You saw God." It was a supposition, not a question.

"No." She finally lifted her gaze to his. "But I saw a field, in summertime, with dandelions waving in the breeze. And I heard a voice. I'd never heard it before or since. It was a man's voice, and at the same time it wasn't. It was loud but not scary. Like it was all around me, wrapped around me, keeping me safe. I can't really describe it any better than that."

She had turned her hand over while telling him, her fingers now linked with his though she didn't seem aware of it.

"What did this voice say?"

"It said, 'I'm not ready to receive you yet, Lisa. You need to go back to your family.' I remember I was crying, at least inside, because it was so beautiful and peaceful. I didn't want to go back. I said so, too, but the voice said, 'I'll be waiting for you when the time comes, but you are not done living, or giving, yet.' "

Roger didn't know if she had seen heaven or if her mind took her to a place that was beautiful and serene to protect her from the trauma of dying and being brought back, but he didn't doubt her story for a minute. He might not subscribe to any formal, organized religion, but he believed in the power of faith and the power of positive energy. Faith could move mountains. In her case, if it brought her back from death, he would be forever grateful.

"What now?" she asked.

"I'm still the same man I was when I walked into the town clerk's office. You're still the same woman."

She exhaled a ragged sigh. "I don't know how we make this work."

"I go to church once in a while. You know, funerals, baptisms, that kind of thing. The roof has never fallen in on me before."

They should have laughed, but neither one did.

"Are you worried about us or about telling your

family?"

"I already told them."

That surprised him. The woman was forthright most of the time, but she had avoided a couple of pretty big discussions with him, so he had half expected her to hide from this one.

"How did that go?"

Instead of replying, she pulled her fingers free of his and turned in her seat to face him. "It was okay." She lifted her chin like a warrior woman going into battle.

He wondered just how hard it had been.

"Hazel helped me."

If he was shocked before, it was nothing compared to now. "The same woman who tried to warn me off? *That* Hazel?"

A smile lit her gaze. "It turns out my little sister can be pretty wonderful. She lost someone once, and she said she doesn't want to see me make the same mistake."

He'd have to reevaluate his opinion of Pastor Hazel.

"She also said she's planning to have a baby."

Now he was speechless.

"No kidding," Lisa said as if she read his thoughts. "She works as a public accountant on the side. Her business has grown enough that she can afford to start a family through artificial insemination and support herself afterward. I'll be the godmother, of course."

"Fairy godmother."

"Right."

They shared a smile, and he imagined her in the pastel cape David suggested, with a wand in her hand to protect a sleeping infant.

"I'm sorry I didn't tell you."

He heard the ache in her soft whisper, matching the one he'd been suffering from since Wednesday morning. "So you're still willing to see me?"

Her nod was hesitant at first. Then, meeting his gaze directly, more certain. "Yes. It might take me a while to figure this out, but my feelings for you haven't changed. Just my image of us."

Chapter Nineteen

They talked every day that week.

"Bryce takes his last final on Thursday," he told her.

Lisa knew that meant his son would be on a month-long winter break and could cover chores for him, but she didn't suggest Roger spend the night, and he didn't ask to.

"Hazel had her first appointment with a reproductive specialist in Burlington yesterday," she relayed during one of their calls. "If all goes well, I'll be an aunt next year."

"I watched a news special about an Ohio farmer with a three-legged cow."

"Guess you're not the only pushover out there."

Though each conversation came easier, they avoided the topic of their future.

On Saturday she gave up her table at a holiday craft fair to work for Maisie.

With Christmas only a week away, people were too busy running last-minute holiday errands to worry about registering their cars. No one came in after eleven thirty.

Preston kept her company for an hour while Gabe caught up on paperwork in the selectmen's office, and Jonnie dropped off a turkey club sandwich from The Common Store, but still the time dragged.

An hour and a half left to go. Watching the clock reminded her of that day in October when she'd waited for the small hand to finally reach two so she could tell her best friend about him. A lifetime ago, yet only eight weeks had passed.

"What makes him the perfect man for you?" Hazel had asked Sunday night while they waited for their parents to answer their call.

"You're probably wondering if it's because he paid attention to me when other men don't. It's okay," Lisa said when her sister would have protested. "I had to have that conversation with myself. You know, is this love or gratitude?"

Pausing, she wondered how to explain what she felt for him. "It's not that he noticed me, personally. It's the fact that he is a man who *would* notice in the first place. I've never met anyone more thoughtful, more observant."

"I understand." A bubble on Lisa's computer screen had indicated their parents were waiting to be admitted to their video call. "And if he makes you happy, then I'm happy for you."

She thought about calling her sister now, for company, but didn't want to test the bonds of their new relationship with too much familiarity.

The irony of that didn't escape her notice. She had known Hazel for thirty-five years and was only now really getting to know her, while she had met Roger eight weeks ago yet felt like she had known him forever. Like he should be in her life every day.

Maybe he was thinking along those same lines, because when she wheeled out of the town offices at two, he was standing on the sloped sidewalk, arms crossed over his chest and back against the railing.

A bright winter sun sparkled on crusted fields of snow in the gap between buildings behind him, but it couldn't compete with the warmth exploding in her chest. From his Canadiens hat to the rubber-bottomed duck boots on his feet, he was all man and all hers.

"Hello, darling."

Her heart climbed up into her throat, and she had to swallow it back down before she could speak. "Fancy meeting you here. Any special reason?"

"Give your keys to Bryce." He unfolded his arms and advanced up the sidewalk to her. "And your wheelchair."

"Why would I do that?"

"So he can drive your car home. I've got a surprise for you."

She swung her footrests out of the way and stood. "I love surprises, you know."

"I know." Grinning, he folded her chair up like an accordion. "Keys?"

"Oh. Right." She fished them out of her crossbody bag and handed them to Bryce, who stood on the other side of the railing. "Thanks, hon."

"You bet." The young man unlocked her car with the button on the key fob, then got into the driver's seat after pushing it back as far as it would go. He managed to squeeze himself into the vehicle with barely enough clearance for his height. Meanwhile Roger lifted her chair and put it in the back seat.

"Ready to go?"

"Absolutely."

Still having no clue what he planned, she took his offered elbow and walked with him across the plowed parking lot to the gap between the Baker Free Library and the volunteer fire department.

"Oh, Roger."

That was the extent of her vocabulary as surprise and excitement robbed her of breath. Two chestnut horses with flaxen manes falling over their faces snorted steam into the cold air and stamped their hoofs in the snow. Each movement made the bells on their harnesses jingle. They were attached to a farm wagon decorated with big red bows, but instead of wheels, the wooden box sat on sleigh runners.

"Your chariot awaits."

He led her to the side, unlatched a small door, and unfolded a set of steps.

Instead of climbing aboard, she took his face in her mittened hands and kissed him. Right there, with the sun for a spotlight and the horses breathing for a serenade.

"I take it you like my surprise?"

"Giddyup, baby."

Laughing, he offered his hand to help her up the steps and, when they were both seated with a red-and-green plaid blanket draped over their laps, asked if she wanted to take the reins.

For answer, she held out her hands.

"Do you know how to drive this thing?"

"Not a clue."

This was the woman he couldn't live without.

He gave her a quick lesson in how to manage the team and the wagon. "I told Buddy Crawford you'd probably want to take the lead, so he made sure we got the most docile pair of horses he owns. Buddy said you could light firecrackers off behind them and the most they'll do is swish their tails."

"So if I want to belt out Christmas carols, they won't make a run for it?"

She sang all around the common. A few people getting into or out of their cars stopped and waved. A couple with their grandchildren joined in on the chorus to "Let it Snow" while Roger admired her joyful talent.

"I love you, darling."

He hadn't planned to say it.

She hadn't expected to hear it, if the myriad of emotions flashing across her face were any indication. The carol ended mid-sentence.

"I've shocked you."

Fisting the reins in her fingers, she blinked several times.

"I'll love you all the days of my life."

She seemed to recover a little, attempting humor. "Just not in the afterlife?"

"I don't know if there is such a thing." He didn't want to hide from her. Better that they face this, head-on. He hadn't known about her religion; she hadn't known his views. He wasn't foolish enough to think everything would work out just because they wanted it to, but he believed it would if they were honest with one another.

"I mean, I want you with me there, too," she confessed. "I don't know if one lifetime is enough after waiting this long for you. I'll miss you."

That was the closest she had come to revealing her feelings for him, and he wanted to beat his chest like a little boy playing king of the jungle. Instead, he reasoned, "If heaven is a happy place, and all your earthly concerns are forgotten, you won't know I'm not there."

"Then you'd better hold me now because I never plan to let you go."

In fact, she invited him in when they reached her house, but Bryce was waiting for a ride back to Crawfords' farm, so he declined.

"I'll see you tonight at the Grange," he reminded her, barely resisting another parting kiss after the first one lingered long enough to make the horses stamp their hooves.

"Do you want me to bring a dish?"

"Nope." Stepping away from her tempting warmth, he said, "I'll have a beef casserole. You just need to come with your *A* game."

Her cooking made an appearance anyway when Preston brought a plate of gingerbread cookies for dessert and bragged to everyone about how he made them at Lisa's house.

"But we still don't know who has the best recipe," he complained to his father and Bryce, seated on either side of him, " 'cause Slick can't make up his mind."

"It was a tie, fair and square."

"How can a tie be fair?"

"Why don't you let them eat the cookies while we sell more tickets?" Darcy suggested, rising from her seat with her money bag and a roll of 50/50 tickets in her hand. "It's going to be a big drawing tonight."

The prize turned out to be just shy of two hundred dollars, and Lisa's number was called, but when Dougie tried to give her the wad of bills, she took back only what she'd spent on tickets and returned the rest. "Give my winnings to Paul Weatherbee."

The crowd grew quiet, everyone likely

remembering how the boy's accident had cleared the room not so many weeks ago.

Roger appreciated her selfless gesture, but he also knew she wasn't rolling in dough. "Are you sure?"

She nodded. "I don't think he's been able to work much since the accident. He can probably use it more than me."

While they were talking, Dougie had conferred with the other officers and announced that Somerset Grange would donate their half of the drawing as well.

Diners clapped their approval. Roger, Gabe, and Buddy Crawford added enough bills to the pile to "top off the prize" at a total of five hundred dollars.

"That was awfully nice of you," Lisa said when he returned to their table.

"I'm only following your lead, darling." He held her hand where it rested on the table, wondering how he was lucky enough to meet this sweet, kind woman. "Paul gives every penny he earns to Dottie. It's just the two of them, and money isn't always easy to come by."

"His father?"

"Flipped a dump truck when Paul was a kid. No life insurance. Dottie's been holding on to that place by the skin of her teeth, too proud to admit she needs help, but it's been in the Weatherbee family since Vermont was a republic, and she wants to leave it to him. She's starting the campground to bring in more revenue but also to give him a reason to stay."

"He'd leave Somerset?" The stricken look on Darcy's face confirmed everything he suspected about her feelings for the boy.

"Probably not, pumpkin. Dottie just doesn't want him struggling if she can help it."

****

Paul wasn't the only one who got an early Christmas present. Lisa was sitting in her pew at church the next morning, marking the hymnal with little tabs of paper for the day's numbers, when Roger slid onto the bench beside her.

"Well, blow me down."

He leaned in, kissed her cheek, and husked, "Is that an invitation?"

She burst out laughing. Hazel glanced up from her conversation with the organist, and Lisa covered her mouth to contain her mirth. "You're a bad boy," she chided.

"Then it's a good thing I'm in church. Now be quiet so we can hear your sister."

The opening hymn was followed by a prayer, lighting of the Advent candles, and a unison reading. Another hymn, a responsive reading, news from the pulpit, and prayer requests from the congregation. The trustees took collection, and a prayer of thanksgiving was offered, then it was time for the sermon.

"No snoring," Roger warned, and she barely stopped another laugh from escaping.

When Hazel finished with the Christmas story, she didn't call for the congregation to rise as usual. Instead, she came out from behind the lectern, took off her reading glasses, and folded them with great care before placing them on the edge of the communion table where the Advent wreath still burned. She stepped down off the dais and stood at the front of the center aisle.

"I'm going to go off script today, and I ask for your indulgence."

Lisa shifted uncomfortably. Her little sister was nothing if not predictable. Every sermon was prepared days in advance, read, reread, and edited to within an inch of its life before she stepped foot inside the church on Sunday morning. She never came unprepared. Never deviated from the program. A glance showed people in the pews waiting patiently for her to continue. Some with mild concern. Some with curiosity.

After a long pause, Hazel lifted her head and spoke. "A good Christian believes they should turn their troubles over to God. Everything will work out according to His plan, and worrying ourselves sick won't do anyone any good.

"In fact, faith demands we turn those troubles over. If we think we can solve them all on our own, we lack faith in His power to give us what we need when we need it."

Hazel pulled her lower lip in between her teeth. Lisa wanted to get up and go to her, because she only did that when she was on the verge of crying. It was something she started when she was four or five years old. Biting her lip kept her from breaking down in tears. She couldn't remember the last time she'd seen Hazel do it.

"Is everything okay?" Roger whispered.

Apparently even he could feel the tension. Or maybe he just noticed her reaction to her sister's unusual behavior. "I don't know," she told him honestly.

"I have to confess I have been weak," Hazel continued. "I have been trying to manage my life, and manage situations, without trusting God to take care of them for me.

"In 1 Timothy, Paul tells us that if we cannot care for those in our own household, those in our own family, we have denied our faith and are worse than an unbeliever. Here I am, every Sunday, encouraging you to read the Word, reflect on its meaning, and put it into practice in your daily life, yet I must admit I've been worse than an unbeliever."

Lisa glanced around at the members of the congregation. The three children who attended with their grandmother were antsy, but they would be no matter what the topic was. A couple of old ladies who didn't hear well but refused to sit up front were quietly snoring in the back pews. Everyone else seemed transfixed by Hazel's admission.

"You all know my sister, Lisa."

Hazel waved in her direction, and she clutched Roger's hand, afraid of what her sister might say.

"You know she comes here every week. Makes food for the potlucks. Decorates the church. Entertains the kids when they have too much energy. And she does it all with a smile. She gives and gives, and then she gives some more. When I was a little girl, I wanted to be just like her."

Lisa barely managed not to gasp. What was she talking about?

"I think I've surprised her, but how could I not look up to someone who was so brave and strong and fun? Our parents coddled her, made me babysit her when she didn't need a sitter, wouldn't let her do things because they were afraid she'd get hurt, and you know what? Lisa simply smiled and adapted and kept going forward. She's stubborn as a mule."

A few people smiled. Beside her Roger chuckled.

"But she had to be. She had to be tough to survive that kind of limiting affection. I've only just realized she never escaped it because, well, I was doing the same thing. Worrying about her. Trying to protect her from harm. Babysitting her all over again.

"Instead of trusting God, knowing He is in charge and looking out for her, I thought I was the only one who could. I've been examining my ways recently, and I'm not proud of what I found. My sister has been a shining light all my life, a bright, happy light in a world that isn't always so positive, and instead of giving her room to shine, I've tried to contain her flame.

"So I'm going to change. And if there is anyone in your life who you are crushing with compassion or killing with kindness, I invite you to examine your ways. Ask yourself if you're trying to manage your life, and your loved ones, instead of turning your cares over to God and letting Him show you the way."

Lisa buried her head in Roger's shoulder so the kids wouldn't see her tearing up.

"Please join me in prayer."

She didn't even hear the benediction. Her ears were still ringing with her sister's words.

"Amen."

****

Christmas the next week was almost anticlimactic following that surprise. She exchanged gifts with Hazel after church, then helped her deliver meals to shut-ins and people who lived alone. In the afternoon Roger picked her up for a meal with his family.

"You didn't tell me the *whole* clan would be here," she said on seeing the front yard filled with vehicles.

"Just seventeen, if Darcy's count is correct."

"You know that girl wouldn't make a mistake about something like this."

They found everyone gathered in the kitchen. Glen leaned against the counter, one arm around Abby's shoulders, while their toddlers squealed with laughter and ran through the house with Bryce and Chelsea in hot pursuit.

Roger's parents sat at the table with Linda, his aunt, and his uncle. Colin, Darcy, Trevor, and Amy were at what Lisa could only think of as the kids' table, playing a board game and arguing over the rules.

"Good, you're finally here," Trevor said when he noticed them by the mudroom door. "Bryce! Get in here!"

The younger, taller brother ducked into the room with a squirming toddler in his arms, followed by Chelsea holding another.

"You're going to need that practice, Uncle Bryce," Trevor said to him, but his gaze was on Roger. "Because Amy and I are having a baby in June."

Turned out Paul and Lisa weren't the only ones getting a Christmas surprise this year.

"My first grandchild," Roger marveled for what must have been the tenth time between his house and hers.

"Exciting, isn't it?"

"You bet. In six months, I'll go from being Pop to Papa." He reached across the truck console and patted her thigh. "Though I'm still up for parenting, round two, if you should ever change your mind and decide to give it a go."

She knew him well enough to know the offer was sincere, but she also knew she was past that age and stage in her life. Instead, she would love Jonnie's children and Hazel's children, and it would be enough for her. "I think I'm good," she told him, unbuckling her seat belt now that they'd reached her house. "But I'm not against *going through the motions* if you'd like to come in for a while."

He killed the engine.

"First, I have a gift for you," she said when they were inside and had removed their outer wear. "Here." At the table she handed him a small package gaily wrapped in blue-and-silver paper that matched her sparkly fingernails.

He turned it over in his hands, held it up to his ear, and shook it, listening for noise. Meanwhile, she was almost bouncing in her chair with anticipation.

"Lemme guess, a box?" he teased, laughing when she poked him in the ribs.

"Keep it up, and I'll take back my invitation." She couldn't wait to see his reaction.

Blue eyes twinkling, he finally put her out of her misery and tore the paper from the package. "I think you and Malachi might be related."

He pulled the box lid open and withdrew the envelope inside, brow furrowed when he saw the contents. "Scratch tickets?"

"Nope."

Grinning, he pulled the thick red-and-white cards from the envelope and flipped them over to look at the front. "Canadiens tickets?"

"Do you know how hard it was to keep those a secret?"

"Come here, you." Not waiting for her to get up, he slid his hands beneath her thighs and pulled her onto his lap. "Now, darling, that's what I call a present. Thank you."

Sometime later they stopped kissing and came up for air.

"I love you, Roger Douglas Plankey."

"And I love you, Lisa…"

"Ann."

"I love you, Lisa Ann Kirkpatrick."

She couldn't control a wince when he bent her at an angle to resume their lovemaking.

"You're hurting?"

"I didn't get all my exercises in this morning, and it's been a long day."

"Can I rub something down for you?"

She considered saying no, but what better way to end Christmas than with a massage from his strong, capable fingers? "You know what? Yes. That would be great."

"Here?"

"No, my back."

"I mean, do you want to sit at the table, or would you be more comfortable lying down?"

A few minutes later she lay facedown on her yoga mat while he dug his fingers into the tense muscles at the base of her spine.

"Keep this up, and you'll put my masseuse out of business."

Half an hour later she was as boneless as a jellyfish and feeling no pain, so limp she needed help getting to her feet.

"Maybe you could return the favor now." He twitched his right shoulder and worked it with his left hand. "This knot in my back just doesn't seem to go away."

"Of course."

She felt bad for not having considered his own aches and pains. He was a farmer, after all, and his day-to-day existence revolved around physical labor. Naturally, he might have some tension even a hot tub couldn't cure.

"Do you want to lie down?"

"No. I can sit." He flipped a dining room chair around, straddled it, and sat with his back to her. "It's above my right shoulder blade." He stacked his hands on the top rail of the chair and rested his chin on them, giving her access to the affected area.

Lisa spread her palms out over his shoulder and felt something hard beneath her fingers. "There is something here."

"Hmm."

She rubbed in a circular motion around the area. "Let me know if anything hurts."

"I will. You don't have to be gentle."

"You're sure?" Although he was probably tougher than her, she didn't want to hurt him. But at his nod, she flexed her fingers and dug into his muscular flesh.

He murmured his appreciation.

"It's weird. Most of the problem is in one area." She walked her fingers closer to that spot. "It's even outlined." When she touched the edge, she heard a distinct crinkling sound, like plastic. "I think there's something on the inside of your shirt."

"What?" He half lifted his head from where it rested, eyes partially open.

"Maybe a tag or something. Hold on." She pulled the bottom of his shirt free from his jeans and slid one hand up between the cotton material and his undershirt. With the fingers of her other hand, she held the cloth down above the bulge so it wouldn't shift away from her. "Definitely something here." Her hand caught the edge of a plastic square, and she pulled. It came loose but not off. "I've almost got it."

With one more tug the offending item broke free, and she dragged her hand back out from under his shirt. A plastic square, covered on both sides with adhesive tape.

"What do you think it is?"

"I don't know."

He lifted his head now, turned around on the chair, and peered at the item in her palm. "Go ahead and open it."

The first layer of tape came away easily. It revealed nothing but another layer, more firmly wrapped around the plastic. She peeled the tape from the opposite side. Same result.

"Maybe you should get some scissors."

"Good idea." She retrieved a pair from her craft room, returned, and took a seat next to him. She made a snip in the corner of the tape, then carefully peeled it away from the plastic.

And stopped breathing. Literally. Her surprised gasp sat suspended in her lungs while she stared at the little plastic tab and the item taped to it.

"Do you like it?"

She could barely see it through the tears filling her eyes. And still she wasn't breathing. Until he placed a palm between her shoulders and gently rubbed. The plastic card trembled in her hand, and he took it from her, pulled the tape completely off, and shook the emerald-cut ring out onto his palm. A peridot surrounded by tiny diamonds. She almost stopped breathing again. Because it was beautiful. Because she didn't dare believe it meant what she thought it did.

He slipped the ring over her blue-and-silver fingernail until it sat snugly on the appropriate finger of her left hand.

"Colors clash." She laughed nervously.

"It matches your eyes."

She raised those eyes to look into his face, afraid of jumping to conclusions.

"I love the color." He wasn't gazing at the jewelry, but at her. "I want to wake up with it every morning. For the rest of our lives, however long we have together."

No way could she contain her tears now. They spilled over her cheeks and dripped off the end of her chin, yet her tongue was paralyzed.

"Will you marry me, Lisa?"

"Yes." Her voice came out in a choked whisper but loud enough for him to hear if the tight hug he pulled her into was any indication.

When her tears stopped, he pulled back and reached behind him for the box of tissues on the table. She used one to blow her nose and dry her eyes.

"Good thing you said yes." He dug into his pants pocket and pulled out a small gray box. "Otherwise, I'd have to take these back." He flipped the cover open to reveal two platinum bands, one thin and feminine, the other thick and masculine.

"But you don't wear jewelry," she remembered, "because it might get caught in machinery at the farm."

He placed the box down on the table and grasped

her shoulders. "I'd lose a finger for you, darling."

"No way." She turned her head and kissed the back of his hand. "We'll get a silicone ring for you."

"You don't have to do that."

"Yes I do. Your fingers are magical, and I plan on you keeping all ten of them."

He puffed out his chest like the male of every species on hearing he'd pleased his mate. "The things you say."

Epilogue

"You didn't tell me labor was that painful." Lisa stretched her legs in front of her and tried to get comfortable in the hospital chair without waking the baby in her lap, cradling her cellphone between her ear and shoulder. "If you did, I must not have been listening."

"Well, what did you think it was going to be?" Jonnie asked. "A walk in the park?"

"No, but you made it seem so easy when you had little Johnny." In fact, her friend had been in and out of the hospital in less than six hours while she and Roger had been here five times as long waiting for this little one to make her appearance. "Boy, am I glad it's over."

"I was worried."

"You were?"

"Sure. Any time labor is three weeks early, that's cause for concern."

"Hmm. I think this girl just wanted to share her birthday with me." Lisa fingered the baby's downy-soft cheek, fascinated with the movement of her lips, the flutter of her eyelashes. "I'm going to have to get started on a Halloween outfit for her for next year. She'll be walking by then, right?"

"Probably. Maybe she can be your flower girl since you had to postpone the wedding due to her premature arrival."

"We're not waiting until the *next* October thirtieth!"

Lisa sent Roger a don't-even-think-about-it look. To Jonnie, she said, "I loved the idea of getting married on the anniversary of our first date, but I've waited long enough already. We'll just have to pick another date. Assuming your calendar is flexible?"

"I'll be there. Now tell me. Does she look like you?"

"Does she ever. She has a head full of curly brown hair just like I did when I was born. I think her eyes are shaped more like Hazel's, though. They say the color is uncertain for the first couple of months, so there's no telling what they'll be by then."

"Sounds like you're in love already."

"Absolutely."

"And Roger?"

"He says if she looks like me, there's no way he'll be able to resist her. But you know how he is with the *gals* in his life." Grinning at him, she added, "He'd love her if she had an eye in the middle of her forehead and fangs for teeth."

"Eww!"

"Gross, right? But you know what I mean."

"And Hazel? How was she through all of this?"

"I was proud of her." The sudden tears clogging the back of Lisa's throat were a surprise.

"Hey." Roger reached over from where he sat in a vinyl visitor's chair and squeezed her shoulder, then glanced at the warm little bundle in her arms, freshly bathed and wrapped in a soft pink blanket. "She's lucky to have you. So is the little one."

Blinking rapidly, Lisa nodded, then said to Jonnie,

"Hazel was amazing. Calm and patient. A real trooper."

"And she's back." Her sister shuffled into the hospital room, hair neatly groomed but dark circles beneath her eyes. She sank into a deep chair next to the bed and put her feet up on the matching footstool. "Mind if I hold Analisa?"

Lisa nuzzled her goddaughter's soft cheek before passing her over, saying, "I think your mommy missed you, sweet pea."

A word about the author...

Amber Cross was raised on a family farm in New England, one of a dozen siblings, each one inspiring her writing in some way. She still lives in that same small town with her husband and the youngest of their five children. She loves spending time in the woods, in the water, and watching people because every one of them has a unique and fascinating story to tell.

~*~

Find Amber online at:
https://www.amber-cross.com/
https://www.facebook.com/AuthorAmberCross

Thank you for purchasing
this publication of The Wild Rose Press, Inc.

For questions or more information
contact us at
info@thewildrosepress.com.

The Wild Rose Press, Inc.
www.thewildrosepress.com